ADDICT

By

Rachael

Orman

Addict

Copyright 2014 by Rachael Orman

All rights reserved. Except as permitted under the U.S. Copyright Act of 1976, no part of this publication may be reproduced, distributed, or transmitted in any form or by any means, or stored in a database or retrieval system, without prior written permission of the author.

The scanning, uploading, and distribution of this book via the Internet or via other means without the permission of the publisher is illegal and punishable by law. Please purchase only authorized electronic editions and do not participate in or encourage electronic piracy of copyrighted materials. Your support of the author's rights is appreciated.

Addict is a work of fiction. Names, characters, places, and incidents are either the product of the author's imagination or are used fictitiously. Any resemblance to actual persons, living or dead, events, or locales is entirely coincidental

Acknowledgements

As always, I owe _everything_ to my one and only, my husband. And to the two little girls who are wonderful at turning my hair gray when they aren't making me pull it out by the handful.

Jacqui - As always the first to get my book, the first to give me support, the first to start messaging on me for more… Love ya lady!

Editing Juggernaut - Thanks for the amazing work you do helping me get my book ready for readers!

Phycel Designs - Amazing cover! Absolutely beautiful and exactly what I wanted but couldn't quite put into words.

Aerii/Andrea/Adrian/AJ - Whatever I feel like calling you today.. Thanks for kicking me in the butt and making me keep writing even when I was having a down day

Chapter 1

Alix

Four nights a week, I sat at my desk off the lobby of the five-star hotel I worked at, waiting for *him*. It never failed; he always showed up.

Flipping my wrist over, I checked my watch. Almost show time. Sitting alone at my desk, I separated my legs, forcing my skirt to climb higher up my thighs. The sensation of the satin lining sliding over my nylon thigh-highs had me biting my lower lip. Excitement pulsed through me, growing with each second that passed. I was ready for him. Just like every night I knew he came in, I had slipped my panties into my purse so I was bare under my skirt.

While I couldn't see the front door from my office window, I didn't need to. Every female head snapped toward the door when he arrived. He simply owned the room from the moment he appeared. From the swagger in his step to the way his observant eyes scanned the area showed he was all he appeared to be and more. His broad shoulders, thick arms and sexy smile only added to his appeal.

As he stepped into my view, I slid my hand under my skirt. Skimming my fingers against my bare, damp flesh, I watched as he approached the front desk. The girl behind the counter jumped to help him, flashing him a smile when he leaned his elbows against the counter. The back of his finely-tailored suit stretched over his flexing muscles while he talked to her.

From my viewpoint I could only see part of his face, but I had watched him enough to have every detail of his face memorized. The crinkle of his cheeks meant he was smiling at her. My teeth dug into my bottom lip as I remembered the times I'd been lucky enough to get a full view of that smile. My fingers dipped between my swollen, needy lips to find the hard, nerve-filled nub nestled there.

As he shifted his feet, his slacks tightened against one thigh and his ass giving me the exact material I needed. My fingers circled and teased my clit. My eyes zeroed in on his well-manicured hands, which were resting on the counter. They were too far away to get a good look at, but it was easy to imagine it was one of those hands between my thighs. Licking my lips, I fought to keep my face passive in case anyone else happened to glance in my direction.

His fingers were long, sensual and always well kept. Most men didn't care about hands, but he did — I did. As he picked up the key card from the counter between two fingers and nodded at the girl behind the desk, I pushed two of my own fingers deep into my pussy. It clenched tightly around my digits as I drank in the sight of him walking.

The top two buttons of his dress shirt were undone, with no tie, no chest hair peeking out — just smooth, muscular skin to feast upon. He strode toward the elevators - toward me.

Thrusting my fingers, I couldn't help but focus on the movement of his hips. Each step only accentuated the slight bounce of his cock behind his dress slacks. Not that his short, light brown hair, brilliant blue eyes or kissable lips took away from my fantasy, but it was the way even his stride was sexy — the way every single thing about him controlled the very air I breathed.

He was my addiction. A man I'd never even spoken to. A man whose name I didn't know. I didn't *need* to know more about him. I was already in deeper than I wanted to admit. Even after three years of not giving into the urges of my addiction to sex and masturbation, there was no thought of not touching myself when I laid eyes on him. Not that he knew who I was or what I did while watching him. That was okay, though. I didn't need to lose my job.

When he stopped to wait for an elevator, I sped up my thrusting, brushing my thumb against my clit as I moved. Biting down on my bottom lip, I held back the moan that threatened to burst from my lips as my release grew close. Just as the orgasm crashed over me, the man lifted his head and locked eyes with me. Unable to stop my fingers, I eased the rest of my release while his eyes burned into mine.

There was no way he could have known what I was doing, but the quirk of one eyebrow made me think differently. I had been careful, but somehow he'd caught me.

His eyes dared me to look away, but I couldn't. Not even when his tongue dragged over his bottom lip, heat flashing in his eyes.

A ding signaled the elevator's arrival and broke our semi-intimate moment.

Turning, he stepped into the elevator, only to turn back around to watch me as the doors closed. The movement of his large hand drew my attention to the front of his slacks as he adjusted his very noticeable, hard cock. My eyes snapped back up to his to find a sexy half-smile on his face. He had done it on purpose.

He *wanted* me to see that he was turned on, that he knew what I had done. Closing my eyes, I withdrew my hand from my skirt and took a deep, calming breath, my heart racing for an entirely different reason than it had been. When I opened my eyes, the doors were closed and the elevator had whisked away the man I dreamt about.

Even before I could come down from the high I got from getting off, I felt shamed. It was wrong. I knew it was. I didn't even know the man. Sure, this time had been different than the many times in the past. He'd noticed me, but I was still at work. I shouldn't even think about sex at work, but I couldn't stop myself. I knew as soon as I got home I would have to do it again. That's *if* I could wait that long. I might take a break before I was done at work and get off in the bathroom.

It was a compulsion. It was an addiction. The path wasn't new to me. I'd already been through the program. I'd been 'sober' or 'on the mend' or whatever you wanted to call it for three and a half years. During that time, I had only had sex with one man. Not even masturbating during that time had been a challenge, but I'd done it.

Everything changed when I first saw *him,* right after my three-year anniversary. It had started as just staring at him from across the room while thinking every naughty thing I wanted to do to a man like him. Slowly, it had progressed into what it was— out of control compulsions. At least five times a day, I got off while thinking of one person, one man. I didn't want anyone else. No one else even made me think of sex.

Why him? I'd thought about it many times, but in the end it didn't matter. My body wanted his in a way that I'd never encountered in almost thirty years of my life. No matter how I tried to fight it, I gave in before I even realized it.

Running my opposite hand through the wavy brown hair that fell to the middle of my back, I knew I needed to get my mind off him and back on work, or I would be fingering myself in the bathroom before long. The only time I ever did it at my desk was when I knew he would be around. Even though I had memorized everything about him, my orgasm was always better when I could see him.

It had been hard not to make a sound when I'd come, his eyes taking it all in —especially knowing he'd been hard. I'm sure he knew what was I was doing — at least had *some* idea — or why else would he have had a hard-on? Fuck, thinking about how large his dick looked even across the room, hiding behind slacks, made my mouth water and my pussy clench. As much as women liked to think there were men walking around packing serious heat, most weren't. Most were just average, despite what they tried to claim — I would know, from the sheer number of men I'd been with — but I knew his had definitely been *big*.

Someone clearing their throat had me crossing my legs and turning my chair. In the door way stood a man and a woman in evening wear. I waved them in to the two vacant seats on the opposite side of my desk.

How silly of me to forget where I was, or the fact that I had an appointment due to show up. Being an event coordinator for the hotel kept me busy most days. There was always something or another that needed to be followed up with, an event to get set up, people to meet with. Thankfully, I didn't do the weddings. I had a single staff member that worked under me and that was all she did. Weddings were dreadfully boring and I was happy to avoid having to see stupidly happy couples together when more than half of them would end up divorced and hating each other in a few years. However, during the busy season, I would have to help her out because it became more than she could handle.

The appointment didn't take long. We only had to go over a few final details for a birthday party being thrown for the couple's oldest child. A huge twenty-first birthday party for a bunch of spoiled brats. I had never been so lucky to get anything half as extravagant as what they had planned for the kid and his friends, but then again, my parents didn't have the money that these parents obviously did.

I was almost thirty. It'd been a long time since I'd lived at home. In fact, my twenty-first had probably been the last birthday I actually celebrated. I didn't have friends to throw me a party, which was okay since I didn't want one anyway. Who wants to celebrate getting old? I was single, no kids, and running out of my so called 'prime' years. I didn't really mind though. What would change in another ten years? Nothing. I'd probably still be at the same job and still single. People like me just didn't get married. Sex addicts never fully recovered. It would always be something I struggled with.

Not to mention that even imagining the fun conversation that would have to take place with a man had me groaning. Seriously, who wants to say, "I might start compulsively wanting to have sex with you or myself"? Nope, not me. It was embarrassing enough to have to deal with it on my own. The only reason I had even realized that I had an issue in the first place had been because I'd gotten fired for masturbating repeatedly at work and watching porn. Not that it had changed anything. I'd crashed after that. Completely hit rock bottom. I spent hours alone playing with myself or finding men to sleep with. That was, until my landlord threatened to evict me if I didn't start paying rent. Sounds crazy, but addiction is addiction is addiction. I lost sight of the real world and what was considered "okay" and "normal". Orgasms had become all that was important to me. There was no one around to help me see what my life had become, not when addiction had first taken over. There still wasn't anyone that cared or would even notice in my life.

I had a mother, a father and a brother around somewhere. We weren't close. I'd go months without hearing from any of them and that was fine by me. We didn't even get along enough to pretend to care about each other.

The only person I had to rely on was myself, and that was how I wanted it. I didn't get lonely. I always had something to do, somewhere to be. Mostly I worked long hours, slept a lot and vegged at home, but it wasn't hard to find something to do on the rare occasion that I wanted to get out for a bit. It was, after all, my job to know what was happening around town so I could plan other events around and between. I didn't care to go out and party. It was easier to stay away from temptation when I was by myself, away from sexy people and sexy thoughts — except the one person who came to me when I was at work. That was one I had a hard time escaping. Maybe that's why I had such a hard time fighting it.

The ding of the elevator brought me back to where I was after yet again getting lost in my thoughts. I looked up. It was the suit man, only he wasn't in a suit. He was in a pair of sexy jeans and a tight-fitting t-shirt. Another standard for him. He always arrived in a suit, but left in a different suit or jeans a few hours later. I had no idea where he was getting clothes from, since he never had a bag of any sort with him when he arrived or left. He never had company with him either, not men or women.

I had closely watched him trying to figure out what his story was, but he never gave anything away. Never talked to anyone in the lobby. Never met anyone outside. It was the strangest thing. He'd come in, stay for a couple of hours, then leave in a different set of clothes, only to arrive the next night in a suit again. At some point he had to come back when I wasn't there. I didn't work all night. It was the only solution I could come up with, anyway.

Many times I had debated about clocking out and staying after just to see if he came back. I had even done it one night, but after working a ten-hour shift, I only lasted two hours before I couldn't wait any longer and had abandoned the idea. I knew it was wrong, yet the desire to know more about him was so strong, I would most likely do it. That is, if I didn't finally get in touch with my doctor and admit that I had relapsed. I didn't want to call him. I didn't want to have to admit it. I knew part of his solution would be to get a different job, one where I wouldn't have to see the man who drove me crazy. *That* was something I wasn't ready to do. Seeing him was what made my mundane life a tiny bit exciting, gave me something to look forward to.

When I looked at my life in that light, it made me realize that I really needed to get out more, needed to find something to help keep my mind occupied and away from that man. Jennifer at the front desk would probably want to go out sometime. Plus she could tell me more about the mystery man, since she was the one who always checked him in and talked to him.

Or maybe spending time with her wouldn't be such a good idea.. Every day when I watched him, I felt myself get more drawn under his spell. It wasn't healthy, but still I couldn't stop myself from yearning to get closer. Knowing more. Like what his voice sounded like, what he smelled like, what the brush of his hands would feel like, the rush of his breath against my neck. I wanted it all.

Chapter 2

John

The night had started out just like any other Wednesday night. After work, I checked into my hotel room while being hit on by the blonde behind the counter — Jennifer, I believe her name was. She always worked Wednesday nights and she tried to get me to ask her out every single week. It didn't matter what she hinted she was into or wanted to do to me. She was too plain in looks and too slutty in personality for me. I'm sure many men wanted her with those perky tits, plump lips and bleached hair, but it was the way she presented herself that was a complete turn-off to me. Perky and giggly did nothing for me. She was a girl — maybe not in age, but in personality. I didn't have time for girls. I didn't even have time for women lately.

My job kept me too busy for the games that came with dating. If I needed release, I knew where I could go. The Scene. It belonged to a buddy from college; I stopped by when the urges became too much to ignore. No boring date, no smooshing, no cuddling. In and out, needs met for both parties and then we went our separate ways. It was simple, it was clean, and it was exactly how I liked it.

When I wasn't working, I was indulging in my addiction. My job and my addiction were contradictions to each other — I'd lose the former if anyone found out about the latter.

My job. Sex therapist. I'd been told I was a pervert or disgusting. If I wasn't being insulted, I was questioned — how could I stand to watch other people have sex? What made me want to do such a gross job? Did I get off from watching and instructing other people? When all was said and done, most people simply didn't understand what I did and didn't give me two seconds to explain it. Sure, I watched people I knew little about do the most intimate things, but I also saved marriages from complete disaster when it was embarrassment or touchy topics that were being avoided. Most of the time it wasn't hard to help find the spice and heat that faded in relationships. Love is driven by lust. All it takes is a little lust to spark love…and as long as that love was still somewhere within, it wasn't hard to find that lust again. If you knew where to look that is.

Did I personally believe in love? No. Not at all. It's just the crap I told my clients and they always ate it up. All *I* needed was control. Being in control of an intimate situation was more powerful and satisfying than if I'd been in the middle of the actual act. I didn't need intimacy to be satisfied — just control.

Not only needed, but craved —thrived on— having it. I did nothing without thinking of how to make sure that I would be in control, that I would be the one making the choices.

A wink and a nod at Jennifer, to let her down nicely, as I gave a short wave with the key card she'd just placed in front of me. I could feel the eyes on me.

I knew exactly who it was that was watching me. She watched me every time I walked into the hotel. Little did she know that I watched her back. I followed her. I craved to one day get my hands on her. The timing had to be just right though.

Turning away from Jennifer, I took a few steps toward the elevator. My ability to stay in the shadows and watch from afar was wearing thin. I needed to get closer. I needed her to see me, want me. Pausing to press the elevator button, I turned to watch my beauty. She might catch me, but I didn't care. It would be hours before I'd be able to see her again.

To my surprise, she wore an expression of complete and utter pleasure. I knew that look. Maybe not from her, but I most certainly knew it from women I'd slept with in the past. She was in the middle of an orgasm and, damn, she wore it well. My dick was instantly hard, throbbing for her — to be the cause of that face.

I couldn't tear my eyes away from her even as her orgasm face left and her eyes burned into mine. I wanted her to be the one to look away. It had to be she who broke the moment.

She didn't.

She held my gaze until her eyes dropped to follow the path my tongue took as I moistened my lips.

When the elevator dinged alerting me to its arrival, I groaned and turned away from her. Thankfully no one else was waiting for the elevator and no one exited when the doors slid open. Stepping inside, I faced her again.

She was still watching me.

I wanted to see just how bold she was so I adjusted my cock, drawing her attention to it — letting her know it had enjoyed her little show. I'd have enjoyed it much more if the damn wall and desk hadn't blocked most of her from my sight.

Her eyes were on my cock for a long moment before they jumped up to meet mine again.

The smirk that crept onto my face couldn't be held back. It was the exact reaction I'd wanted. The message had been received loud and clear.

The doors slid shut before she recovered, but that was okay. I had other matters that I needed to focus on. The little interlude in the lobby had been unexpected, yet I would remember it for a long time.

Leaning against the side of the elevator, I closed my eyes and let it take me to the top floor. My apartment. It hadn't been cheap to get the hotel to allow it, but it was necessary with the type of business I had. I made good money from my clients and was able to afford it. It was convenient to have my place only floors above where my clients normally met me, and the building my office was in was just next door. Sometimes I met clients at their own places, so I had my car in the hotel's underground garage.

Once the elevator opened on my floor, I used my key to unlock the door. From the outside there was nothing to distinguish it from the other rooms in the hotel. Inside, however, it was completely different. I had renovated it to have a master suite, a small kitchen, tiny living room, good sized office, and a spare room with extra bathroom. It wasn't *huge*, it wasn't all that impressive when it came to decorations. It was simple, it was conveniently located right in the middle of my world, so it worked. No one ever came to my place. Not friends, not women. It was my space.

The majority of my time was spent working. When I wasn't with clients, I still had plenty of work to take care of, not to mention I worked a few nights a week as an online therapist. It helped fill the hours. Downtime wasn't something I enjoyed. Being busy, being successful, *that* was what I enjoyed.

Making the short walk through the apartment, I
tossed my suit coat on the bed before entering the large
walk-in closet. The one thing I'd made a requirement in
my living quarters. I had a lot of clothing and I spent a
lot of money on it, so naturally having space to keep it
was a top priority. Looking anything but my best wasn't
an option. No one wanted to accept advice from
someone who looked sloppy, especially advice in the
bedroom department.

I slipped off my dress shoes and put them back
where they belonged before stripping down to my
briefs. All of my clothing was laundered by the hotel. It
was pricey, but again, it was easier than dealing with it
myself or taking it elsewhere. My slacks were tossed
onto the small mound of clothing that hadn't been
picked up yet. The white dress shirt followed.

Knowing the clients I was meeting with next, I
pulled on jeans and a t-shirt. I had a few minutes before
my appointment, so I powered up my laptop to check
my emails and review the client files, although I knew
the couple quite well. As I figured, there wasn't
anything surprising that I'd forgotten since the last time
I'd met with them.

Bridgette was a trophy wife who wasn't afraid to
step outside of their marriage to find what was missing
in the bedroom. Even after being turned down numerous
times, she still hit on me every time she could without
her husband seeing. Mike, on the other hand, was a
smart-looking older man. He knew what his much-
younger wife was up to, but he put up with it as long as
she gave him what he wanted, when he wanted it. After
months of meeting with them, I wasn't entirely sure why
they insisted on continuing to meet with me. They were

quite possibly the most tame couple on my client list, with fairly normal request and desires. Part of me, though, knew they liked the feeling of voyeurism that came with having someone outside of your marriage watch as you acted out intimate desires.

Deciding that I'd wasted enough time, I headed down to the rented room I used for clients. I normally rented the same room, but not always, sometimes I required two rooms or had clients that met close together so I needed rooms that were nearby each other… so I would take whatever was available at that time. Although a majority of the time, I got this room, which I preferred as it was near the stairwell and gave an quick escape if necessary for any reason. As expected, the room was perfectly cleaned and ready for my appointment. Before I could even settle into the armchair to wait, there was a soft knock on the door.

When I opened it, I was greeted by Bridgette in a tiny black dress and entirely too much makeup.

"Please, come in." I stepped back and gestured for her to enter.

"Hello, John," Bridgette purred, dragging her nails across my chest as she strutted into the room. "How have you been?"

"Fine. Please, take a seat." I moved back to the armchair leaving the love seat for her.

Exaggeratedly rolling her hips, she tried her best to look sexy as she made her way to the seat I indicated for her. "Anything for you, baby."

Completely unaffected, I watched her without reacting. Once she finally sank down onto the love seat, I sat forward, resting my elbows on my knees. "How have things been with Mike?"

"Oh, I can think of *so* many other interesting things we can do to get me ready for my husband's arrival besides talk." She lowered her voice an octave and spread her thighs.

"The only think I want to talk about is your husband and how your relationship has been." It wasn't her. I simply wasn't into fucking married women. It was bad for business and too complicated to be worth it.

Standing up, Bridgette slipped her dress over her head to reveal her bare tits and a sheer thong. Her manicured hands cupped her fake breasts as she stepped closer to me. "Come on, big boy."

"No." Pushing out of the chair, I grabbed both her wrists. With a little effort, I had them clasped behind her back, her chest against mine. "Not interested," I growled in her ear.

"Mmm. Yeah, grab me. Force me to do what you want me to do." Biting down on her lip, she tried to nuzzle my neck, but I stepped back, turning her away from me at the same time. The quick move had her stumbling, but my grip on her wrists balanced her. She cried out and yanked on her arms. "What the fuck is wrong with you?"

"I told you. Not. Interested. I've made it clear in the past, but this is the final time." Lowering my mouth to her ear, I spoke in a threatening tone of voice, "Pull something like this again and I'll make sure your husband gets hard proof of the *many* times you've made advances on me."

"I'll tell him you were the one hitting on me," she sneered, attempting to free her hands again.

"Oh, please. Do you think I'd be stupid enough not to make sure I had precautions set up for such a thing?" I released her hands and stepped back from her.

Turning, she shrugged and finger-combed her hair as if she weren't still mostly nude.

"Fine. Whatever. He would've never known. Plus, I only wanted to have you unleash all…" She trailed off and dragged her eyes over my body from head to toe and back again before adding, "All *that* with that controlling shit you just did. Fuck yeah."

A knock on the door alerted me to the arrival of her husband. "So, that's what does it. I'll give Mike some pointers. On the bed." I nodded at it before moving to open the door.

"John," Mike acknowledged as I let him into the room.

When we both turned to look at the bed, Bridgette had herself spread eagle on it. Her wrists were near the head of the mattress on either side, feet spread wide. From the bulge in Mike's pants, he was enjoying the view.

Letting the door shut on it's own, I smiled. "Well, Mike, I have some good news to share with you."

Mike met my look with a wary one. "What's that?"

"I think I made a breakthrough with your wife tonight." I walked to one side of the bed and pulled the thick strap that I kept there from under the mattress. "Your wife would like to be restrained. Tied down and fucked hard."

Mike cleared his throat. "I've never done anything like that before."

"And that's why I'm here. Come, I'll show you exactly how to do it." I quickly showed him how to tie the rope and how to quickly untie it to release her. Once

I restrained one wrist, I let him do the other one. "Now…she's all yours."

I stepped back and watched as Mike trailed his fingers over her stomach, making her shiver and tug at the rope. Slowly, he literally kissed Bridgette from head to toe, which had her moaning and squirming. When he sucked her big toe into his mouth, my eyebrow jumped in surprise. Hadn't seen that coming as most men — hell, most *people* — avoided the feet on their partner. Quickly I schooled my features and leaned a shoulder against the wall, crossing my arms.

My job was over for the most part. I just stuck around to make sure no one got hurt or things went wrong and someone felt taken advantage of when the fun ended.

Bridgette was apparently enjoying the foot bath as her moans grew in volume. By the time they finally progressed to the fucking, I figured it was Bridgette's bold personality that hindered a man like Mike from expressing his desire to try new and somewhat unusual things. A little rope had leveled the playing field for them.

Waiting for the happy couple to find their completion from sex, I let my mind wander to all the silly questions I'd been asked by clients through the years.

Did I get turned on from watching other couples have sex? No. I couldn't think of one time where I even got slightly aroused. It was my job and I acted as such. Was I a pervert? Probably. Not because of my job though. That would have been much more based in what I did when I was off the clock — on my own time, so to speak. Was I gay? That one always made me laugh. Because I wasn't turned on from watching a straight couple have sex, I must be a homosexual. No, it didn't matter how many times or ways I tried to explain it was about control, people didn't understand. Had I ever joined in with my patients? That was one I never would answer — not to a client, friend or anyone. In truth, I had   joined in on the fun, in the past, but it was a very, very rare thing and easier to say no to people than to explain that the chances of it happening were slim to none.

What I wouldn't talk to clients about was what I did in my own bedroom. The things I enjoyed would have most of them running for the hills. Especially the thoughts that surrounded the lovely little Alix downstairs.

Chapter 3

Alix

It had been two days since I'd last seen the mystery man. Not by choice, that's for damn sure; not even my own embarrassment could keep me from wanting to see him. He hadn't shown on Thursday, like he usually did. It was past the time he normally showed on Friday, but there was no sign of him.

Instead of being excited to escape work when that time rolled around, I found myself loitering around the front desk engaging Jennifer in conversation. We'd exchanged small talk about how each other's day had been, and that awkward lull in the conversation that I dreaded was coming. Trying to think up an excuse to give her as to why I wasn't rushing out the door like most people, I inadvertently missed a question.

"What are your plans for the weekend?" Jennifer repeated, leaning forward on the counter. She lowered her voice and glanced around the lobby, making sure no one was within listening range. "I know of this totally exclusive party going on later. You should come with me. I was supposed to go with a couple of my girlfriends, but the bitches ditched me last-minute for some stupid boy band concert."

"Uh… I don't know. I'm not really much of a party-goer." Sighing inwardly, I didn't want to admit to her that I could count on one hand how many times I'd even gone to a bar for a drink, alone or with friends. It just wasn't my thing.

Frowning, she pushed off the counter and folded

her arms across her chest. Sticking out her bottom lip and looking up at me through her eyelashes, she gave me her best pouty face. "Please? I really want to go. I'll do whatever you want. *Anything*. I'll owe you a *huge* favor. *Please*."

I eyed her while internally debating. I didn't know her all that well, but she was always really friendly. I didn't have anything else planned. Then again, I didn't go out much partly because I had problems talking to people in crowds. The perfect excuse not to go suddenly popped into my head. "Even if I went all the way home, I don't even own club attire. It's work clothes or lounge wear for me. Neither seems appropriate for a party." Before I had the chance to mentally pat myself on the back for thinking fast, she scoffed and waved away my excuse.

"You can come to my place and borrow some of my clothes for the night. That's no reason to worry! I have a whole closet that'll fit you! You're, what, a size twelve-ish?" Clapping her hands together in excitement at the sigh of defeat I gave, she bounced on her toes. "So you'll go?"

Taking a deep breath, I rubbed my forehead. "Sure. What time?" I didn't really want to go, but it hadn't been that long ago that I'd been thinking I needed to make friends. Plus, who knew, maybe a change of scenery would be what I needed to get Suit Man off my mind for a bit.

Letting out a squeal that made my ears want to bleed, Jennifer jumped up and down. Her large breasts bounced with the movement and I couldn't help but watch them for fear they were going to burst through her work shirt.

Talking a mile a minute, gesturing wildly with her hands, she started moving around behind the counter. "Right now, well, after work, but I get off in, like, five minutes so that's almost now. I can't tell you how excited I am that you agreed. I've been looking forward to this party for *weeks*. Now I just have to figure out what we're going to dress you in."

Even though I tracked her with my eyes, I couldn't keep up with her rapid speech. Her mouth kept moving even as she gathered a few small items off the counter, shoving them into a purse she pulled from a cabinet under the desk.

Walking around the counter, she looped her arm around one of mine and waved at the woman that worked the counter at night. Trying to keep up with her, I stumbled along as she made a stop to let the manager know she was leaving. After the brief pause, she proceeded to pull me towards the front door of the building. "You know how long I've been trying to build up the courage to ask you to come out with me?" Jennifer continued.

I hadn't been able to keep up with most of her chattering. Thankfully the chilly air outside seemed to slow her speech and speed. I nodded even though I wasn't entirely sure what she was talking about. I wasn't used to someone talking so fast, and definitely wasn't used to someone pulling me around by the arm while doing it.

"If you knew, then why didn't you say something silly?" She stopped walking and gawked at me. Laughing loudly, she slapped playfully at my arm and shook her head as if I'd made a joke.

I shrugged in reply hoping it'd give me a pass. I needed at least ten cups of coffee to get up to the same speed she was at.

"Seriously, girl, you have got to learn to speak up. You sit there in your office all day looking out at everyone. We all wonder if it's because you're shy or if you think you're better than the rest of us. I've always been on your side, saying that you're just shy. I can tell when you talk to customers that you're a total blast to hang out with though. I'm *so* glad you agreed to come out with me tonight," Jennifer continued, once again grabbing me by the arm and leading me towards the section of the parking garage that was sectioned off for employees only.

I wasn't sure how to react to the bit of information she'd just laid on me. I had never in my life been called stuck-up; that wasn't me at all. I had never been called a blast to hang out with either. Feeling a bit put off by the whole direction of the conversation, I frowned and slowed my pace.

"You aren't changing your mind, are you? You can't! I won't allow it. Look, there's my car," Jennifer continued, as if being near her car made it impossible for me to back out. Before I could even respond, she was opening the passenger door of her tiny red sports car and walking around it to get in the driver's side. Having gotten that far, I forced myself to sit in the passenger seat. After pulling the door closed, I made sure to buckle in. If she drove anything like she talked, I'd need it.

After a short, thankfully silent drive, we pulled up to a small house. Jennifer jumped out of the car, slamming the door before hurrying toward the front door. As she reached the pathway through the yard, she glanced over her shoulder and shouted, "Come on."

I got out much more slowly, not nearly as enthusiastic about the night as she seemed to be. Excited, maybe. Curious, yes. Nervous, absolutely.

Once inside the house, Jennifer ushered me to her room and threw clothes at me from the closet so quickly I could barely catch them. I didn't own half as many clothes as she tossed out. Taking the arm-ful of items she thought would look good on me, I made my way across the hall to the bathroom. I set the clothes on the counter and locked the door. Leaning against it, I was finally able to take a deep breath. What the hell was I doing? I never went to parties. I never went out with anyone, period. Change was good though, right? Maybe it was time to learn to step out of my comfort zone.

Giving myself a pep talk and knowing it'd be hell to get out of going, I slipped off my clothes and tugged on a skin-tight, neon pink dress that was on the top of the pile. Closing my eyes, not even chancing a glance in the mirror, I flung open the door and let Jennifer give her opinion. I doubted I'd like the way anything looked on me so it was up to her to decide. As long as I could sit without flashing people and walk comfortably, I could survive a few hours dressed in just about anything.

Jennifer slowly tilted her head side to side as she mashed her lips together. After a moment of contemplation, she shook her head and I retreated into the bathroom for another outfit.

After numerous disappointing ensembles, I became frustrated, not to mention as sweaty as if I were working out. Finally, though, Jennifer's eyes lit up and an enthusiastic nod with two thumbs up let me know that I was done trying things on. She disappeared into her room only to return with a pair of peep-toed five-inch heels. Now *those* were something I could easily do. I wore heels to work every day, so the height didn't bother me. I might not be used to wearing a tight dress that emphasized every curve I had, but I knew that I had nice legs, especially when I wore heels.

Gathering my courage, I took a deep breath and turned to look at myself in the mirror. I released a breath of relief at my reflection. It wasn't as bad as I had expected. Perhaps it was the glint of determination that shimmered in my eyes or the cut of the dress, but it looked like it had been made just for me. Either way, we decided that the dress was what I was wearing and I was okay with the choice.

"Beautiful. I knew you had a luscious, curvy body under those boring work clothes you always wear. I wish I was   as tall as you." Jennifer pulled my hair over my shoulders as she smiled at me in the mirror. She was only a few inches shorter than my five foot seven so I didn't understand what the big deal was. It took her only a few minutes to put spiral curls in my hair, then she slapped on some make-up "to make your eyes pop" as she said. Lacing her arm through mine, she pulled me out of the house. "We are going to draw so much attention," she squealed excitedly as she locked the front door.

I knew she would for sure. Her pleather dress left little to the imagination. It wasn't see-through, but it may as well have been. She continued to talk about how excited she was for the party and how she'd barely managed to get an invitation *this month*. Apparently it only happened once a month, and only those with an invitation could get in. From what I caught, she had slept with a man who got her an invitation. She'd said much more, but I'd barely managed to catch bits and pieces as she drove manically through the city. Finally she turned off the main streets and slowed.

Parking in a dimly-lit lot, she wiggled her eyebrows at me before climbing out of the car. I followed suit, swallowing hard when there seemed to be no one around.

"This way." Jennifer waved over the roof of the car at me to head in the direction opposite of where I had been looking.

Mentally shaking my head at my unwarranted fear, I saw a line to get into a building that had absolutely no signs on the exterior. It appeared to be a warehouse. Once around the car, she looped her arm through mine before taking off toward the building. The line moved quickly and soon we were allowed access through the double doors after handing over Jennifer's invite. Inside I was surprised to find a small desk with a woman in a floor-length gown was waiting.

"Bags, please," she said in a soft voice as she held out both her hands.

I glanced at Jennifer, who met my gaze before shrugging. We both handed over our purses.

"Phones?" the woman questioned with a quirked eyebrow.

"In there." Jennifer pointed to her purse and I nodded.

"You may enter." Reaching an arm back, she pulled open a thick curtain for us to pass through.

Unsure of exactly what the hell I'd gotten myself into, I slowly stepped through behind Jennifer. She reached back to clasp her hand with mine, making sure I stayed with her. The curtain whooshed closed behind us as my eyes roved the room trying to take it all in.

There were multiple stations around the room with people in various states of undress. Many places to sit were also situated around the room. I didn't know what to make of it all. It felt like my brain simply shut down as I stood and gawked.

"Close your mouth!" Jennifer shook my arm fiercely. "This is so awesome. I had heard it was a total kinkfest but I didn't actually believe it."

"You knew we were coming to a party where people were naked? Why didn't you tell me? Did your friends know? Is that why they didn't want to come?" I whispered angrily to her.

"I glossed over it because I knew you'd back out. I didn't want to come alone." She quickly tugged me to the side when the curtain was pulled open again to allow someone else in for the festivities. Once the couple moved into the room, she cleared her throat and gave me an apologetic look. "Don't be mad, but my friends were never coming."

I wanted to be upset that she'd lied, but instead I felt a serene feeling settle over me. Something deep inside me —something I wasn't even aware had been locked up — felt like it had finally been set free. Seeing people tied up, being spanked, on leashes, doing sexual activities out in the open would probably feel awkward to most people. While at first it shocked me, the more I let it sink in, the more natural it felt. Going out with Jennifer had been an attempt to get me out of the sexual haze I normally lived in; instead it felt like I'd found the crowd I should have been spending my time with. People who would understand my desires and obsessions more than so-called normal people would. I'd never participated in anything like the BDSM-type activities around us, well except a little spanking. It'd been something I'd been curious about, but had no idea where to even dip my toe in. Jennifer had found it for me, apparently.

"Let's go walk around." Jennifer yanked on my arm, having gotten her bearings somewhat. However, the closer we got to everyone, the more she gawked. The more comfortable I felt, the more frightened she appeared to get. As we neared the first stage, she pulled me closer to her. Her lips brushed my ear as she whispered hoarsely in my ear. "Do you see that? It's a man… and another man."

"Okay?" I lifted the shoulder she was practically wrapped around, showing I was indifferent to it.

"But he's *whipping* the other man."

Chapter 4

John

Gabe, my buddy who owned The Scene, called in a favor when his younger sister fell ill and asked that I watch his club for a few days. I had done it in the past when he needed someone he could trust to keep an eye on things. He knew that I was in the lifestyle, that I'd know what to look out for in the play room. I didn't frequent BDSM clubs the way I had in my younger years, but not much had changed so it wasn't hard to pick up on who needed to be watched.

He had a good system set up, but with the monthly open party happening, things had to be notched up to keep everyone safe. I had only been to one monthly party over the years. It didn't appeal to me to mingle with a bunch of people who just wanted to dabble in the scene or people who were new to the area, but I could handle watching from the control room's security cameras. I preferred people who knew how the club operated and knew that I was only there for the power exchange, not sex.

Over the month, Gabe and a few other trusted members handed out invites to people they thought would be a good addition to the club or would be interested in joining. Other than the one night, there were no openings to non-members unless they were invited by a member and were in that person's care while in the club. The parties were meant to bring in fresh faces and help keep things interesting with new partners to play with. Private rooms were off-limits during the parties to help ensure everyone was behaving and consensual. Just one more layer of protection for people who didn't understand what it was they were agreeing to.

Of course, everyone got a thorough explanation of what the club was and what would be happening at the party before they were given the invitation, but seeing and hearing are two very different things to most people.

Centering a new camera view on the main screen in front of me, I spotted *her*. Alix. Watching as she walked around the room with the girl from the front desk, I saw the spark of excitement and interest clear as day in her eyes. My cock jumped to attention from the look alone. Front desk girl looked like she was in over her head. She wouldn't be getting a return invitation. It obviously wasn't her scene, but Alix — *she* would be getting one. I'd see to it. She definitely had a naughty streak in her and I wanted to explore it now that I knew she was interested in the same things I was.

With as many cameras as there were, I was able to watch as the pair meandered through the room, taking in the various scenes that were taking place. Multiple times Alix's eyes returned to a couple on the St. Andrew's cross. Did she like being spanked? Or was it being tied up that interested her? My throbbing cock demanded I find out. Instead, I kept watching, following her as she got more and more turned on. Her nipples were beaded, pressing out against her dress. When the women eventually found a set of chairs to sit in, I fisted my hands on my own chair, forcing myself to stay where I was. Alix was rubbing her thighs together. I knew what she was doing even if she thought she was being secretive. I'd bet anything that her pussy was drenched and aching for relief. Rubbing her thighs together, massaging her clit with her pussy lips, she was being a very naughty girl.

After a few moments, she stood and waved the front desk girl off before walking towards the hallway where the bathrooms were. Switching cameras, I followed as she slipped into one of the stalls. There weren't supposed to be cameras in bathrooms, but it was a safety precaution more than anything. There wasn't anywhere in the entire club that someone could be pulled and escape being watched.

From the camera's angle I could see the top of her head. Even feeling like I might be going a step too far, I couldn't convince myself to go back to watching other cameras. When her head snapped back, her mouth wide open, eyes clenched tightly shut, I knew exactly what she was doing.

Before I could think better of it, I pushed the chair back and quickly moved down the hall. Slipping through a locked door, I waited in the dark corner of the hallway. The bathroom door slowly opened and she walked out.

Stepping close, I slid one hand over her mouth and the other around her waist, pulling her firmly against my chest. Not giving her time to scream, I lowered my lips to her ear. "Don't scream. I don't want to hurt you. Understand?"

She nodded after a moment.

Gliding my hand over her chin, I cupped her neck, making her tilt her head up and away. I didn't want her to see my face, didn't want her to know who I was. "I know what you just did, you naughty girl. Why did you do that?"

"Uh…" she stuttered and swallowed hard against my hand. "I don't know what you're talking about?"

Keeping my tone low so as not to be overheard or draw attention, I dragged my nose up the column of her neck. "You were in there playing with yourself. Weren't you? Don't lie to me."

"Y..yes," she said softly.

"Yes, what?" I pushed.

"Yes, sir?" she guessed.

"Hmmm. Yes, that's right." I hummed against her hair, breathing the scent in deep.

"Who are you?" She shifted her feet restlessly, but didn't try to fight my grip on her.

"An admirer. Precious, tell me what is your name?" I knew her name, but I wanted her to know that I knew it. She would be mine. All rules had flown from my mind the moment I'd seen her in the club.

"A… Alix, sir."

"Is that short for Alexandra?"

"No, sir. Simply Alix," she answered without hesitation.

I was surprised she wasn't fighting me at all or asking more questions. She was a natural submissive, if only I had known earlier. I did know it wouldn't be long before her friend came looking for her. It was hard to release her now that I finally had my hands on her.

"Meet me here tomorrow if you want to learn more about what you've seen here tonight. Show up here. Same time. Tell them at the front that you are here for Master J." Inhaling her scent once more, a rumble escaped my chest that sounded suspiciously like a purr. With a nip to her earlobe, I pulled away, slipping back into the same door I'd just used before she could respond.

I'd give her all day to think about whether she really wanted to explore the BDSM lifestyle. I wasn't going to do anything to convince her as it had to be her decision, not mine.

Resuming my position in front of the cameras, I watched as she stood in the hallway taking slow, deep breaths as she leaned back against the door I'd disappeared through. To my delight, she slipped a hand under her skirt right there. Her fingers nimbly moved her panties to the side so they could assault her clit. After only a few rough, hard rotations, something in the hallway caught her attention and she rapidly pulled her dress back in place. The woman who had disturbed her barely glanced at her before disappearing into the bathroom.

Alix shook her head and even through the camera I could see the fact that she was upset that she'd almost been caught. Wiping her hand on her dress, she scurried down the hall to find her friend. Once she was sitting in her chair again next to the girl from the front desk, she kept her eyes down, no longer as fascinated by what was going on around her.

Not entirely sure what had changed, I continued to watch until she motioned to the door and the pair left the club. I knew they'd be given back their items once they passed through the curtain. Normally if they were to be invited back, I would call the front desk and let them know to slip a return invite into the woman's or man's belongings. I didn't need to with Alix since she had personally gotten her invite from me. All I had to do was sit and wait to see if she showed up.

**

The morning passed incredibly slowly. All I could think about was whether or not Alix would show up. It didn't help that I didn't have any clients scheduled until early afternoon. I had the first hours of my day blocked off to do online counseling. Not the most interesting way to pass the time, but it was a convenient and anonymous way for patients to seek help when they might not otherwise. Normally after a session or two online, I would try to get them into the office so we could speak in person, as it was easier for me to tell what a patient was thinking when I could see their face and hear their vocal intonations.

Finishing up one session, I had an alert that a new client was looking for someone to talk to. Looking at the IP address, I instantly knew who it was. Alix. I shouldn't know such things about her, but I did. I'd been watching her a while. A click later I had a new chat window popping open.

Counselor21: Good morning. This is Counselor21. How are you today?

BadKitty2: Stressed.

Counselor21: What has you stressed?

BadKitty2: What doesn't have me stressed?

Counselor21: Let's start with the most pressing matter and then we'll work our way through them all one at a time.

BadKitty2: Well, I think I'm falling back into my patterns of addiction.

Counselor21: How long have you been clean?

BadKitty2: I've never been clean, doc. On the wagon? Three years.

Counselor21: What do you think is making you jump off the wagon, or start dragging a foot behind the wagon perhaps?

BadKitty2: There's this man. I don't know his name, but I have an unexplainable draw to him.

Counselor21: What type of addiction are we talking about?

BadKitty2: Sex. Masturbating. Release. Getting off any possible way I can.

Counselor21: Is it just this one man that makes the urges stronger and harder to fight off?

BadKitty2: Yes. Just him.

Counselor21: Is that how it was before? Just a single trigger?

BadKitty2: No. Before it didn't matter at all. That is why it's so frustrating and confusing.

Counselor21: How well do you know this man?

BadKitty2: Not at all. I don't even know his name.

Counselor21: Does he know you?

BadKitty2: Possibly by sight.

Counselor21: Can you avoid him?

BadKitty2: No. He comes to the place where I work. I can't get another job for the pay I make. I've already considered it and looked into it.

Counselor21: What about this man makes him different than other men?

BadKitty2: It's hard to explain. The air about him. The way he walks. I just know he could take control of me and do everything naughty I have in my mind without thinking twice about it.

Counselor21: And what do you do when you see him?

BadKitty2: Touch myself.

Counselor21: Do you orgasm while doing it?

BadKitty2: Every time.

Counselor21: And you do this while at work?

BadKitty2: Yes.

Counselor21: What would happen if you got caught?

BadKitty2: I'd get fired.

Counselor21: Does that worry you?

BadKitty2: Yes, but not as much as the urge and need to masturbate.

Counselor21: Have you tried not to give in to those thoughts?

BadKitty2: Doc. I've been down this road before. I try everything, but it's like a smoker trying to quit. They are all on board until that need kicks in and then it's all they can think about until they give in and smoke again. That's exactly what it's like. It becomes all-consuming and as soon as I reach completion, I feel guilty that I caved in yet again.

Counselor21: Would you be willing to come in for an in office visit? We need more time than we have on here to talk.

BadKitty2: No. I can't. Its too embarrassing.

Before I could respond again, she was gone. Running a hand over my face, I sighed. Well, that had been interesting. Even after all the time I'd spent watching her, learning about her life, I hadn't found that incredibly interesting history. When I'd been given my choice of sign ons, I'd picked 21. Simple. For many reasons that number was meaningful in my life. 21, legal drinking age. 21, also, the number for doggie style, my favorite position. I never wanted a woman to face me, I didn't need her face, I simply needed her body. But that was about me, I should've been thinking about Alix, officially my new client.

Sexual addiction was a tough issue. So many people thought it was a joke and not nearly as serious as it could become. Seeing as she had already been through the program once, she knew what she had to do. It was my job to simply help her get her head back in the game and find the tools to resist again. Keeping myself impartial was going to be the challenge. Looking at the clock, I closed the laptop. It was time for my appointment.

Taking the elevator down a few floors, I let myself into the room I normally used. A quick look around let me know the room was ready.

Anthony and Megan were a young couple that, unlike most of my couples, never had a *good* sexual past. They were always on different wave lengths when it came to being intimate, but everything outside of the bedroom was great. When they first came to see me, they had come in because they were afraid lack of passion was going to affect their ability to get pregnant. After six months of trying, they hadn't been successful so they hoped making it more pleasurable for both of them it would also increase the possibility of getting pregnant.

I didn't know about all that. They say when both partners experience an orgasm during sex it helps sperm in some way. Not my department. The last thing I wanted was a baby so I did what I always did. Found a way to make both of them happy. Most of my patients were more afraid to share their deepest, darkest desires with their partner than having actual physical or mental issues that kept them from being able to perform.

After having a quick meeting with each of them, I let them have at it. Megan had wanted to have Anthony be more dominant in the bedroom. Anthony didn't want to hurt his wife, not at all. Baby steps, one thing at a time, I'd told him. Leaning against the wall, I watched as they fucked doggy style. Anthony gathered her hair in his fist, tugging back slightly.

"More," Megan moaned in response.

Anthony looked over his shoulder to gaze at me, stopping all movement. His eyes were wide and wild as if he didn't know how to.

Stepping up to the side of the bed, I grabbed his free hand and put it on her shoulder, then wrapped my hand around the one that was filled with her hair and pulled ever so slightly back.

"Hold her shoulder, pull her back to you. Don't be afraid to slowly pull harder on her hair. Her moans will tell you when you've reached her threshold," I instructed him as he started to thrust again. I returned to my position against the wall. While seeing people have sex didn't bother me, most of them didn't like it when I stood too close.

I zoned out, thinking of what my night was hopefully going to bring. It would be nothing like the tame, slow, loving caresses and fucking that was playing out in front of me. However, it did make my cock twitch excitedly in my pants. The simple thought of getting my hands on Alix had the corners of my lips curling. I shoved away the images of her tied up that were floating through my mind, making me anxious for the rest of the day to pass. It would come soon and I'd finally get the chance to intimately know the enticing brunette.

Chapter 5

Alix

As Jennifer and I had sat taking in the various acts around the room, I couldn't stop thinking about touching myself. I hadn't had the urge to do that without having mystery man on my mind since I'd gotten out of rehab. Shifting in my seat, I tried adjusting my legs, but all that did was make my swollen lips rub against my pulsing clit. No matter where I looked, there was a sexual act taking place. I couldn't escape my thoughts, the need that burned through my body. Finally I couldn't take it any more and excused myself from Jennifer. I couldn't very well have her come with me to the bathroom when I went to release the built-up tension.

Once in the bathroom, I quickly locked myself into one of the small stalls and rubbed my clit fast and hard. I didn't want it to feel good, I didn't want it to leave me gasping and wanting more. I just wanted the thoughts to subside and let me regain control over myself.

Coming to the club had been a bad idea. I should never have agreed to go out. Then again, I didn't know we would be going to a club where people were being spanked and tied up. Although it was like walking into a real version of many of my dreams, I couldn't control my thoughts and desires, couldn't keep them from spinning wildly down the path I fought so hard not to go down again.

Adjusting my dress, I washed my hands and peeked into the hallway to make sure no one might have overheard me. I hadn't yelled out with my release, but I was jumpy after having given into my need for release in a public place. It wasn't the act, especially considering there were people doing much naughtier things in the open. It was the fact that I'd hidden it and felt ashamed of what I'd done. Just as I was stepping out, large hands wrapped around my mouth and waist, pulling me against a hard body. Panic rushed through my body in an instant, until the sexy, hoarse, British voice spilled down my neck. Although his hands held me firmly, they didn't hurt, didn't grope — simply kept me in place.

He knew what I had done in the bathroom. How? I didn't know. Didn't matter, I was too embarrassed to argue when he didn't believe my initial nervous denial.

Making me call him sir had my knees weakening. I might call men "sir" daily, but it was different when the man holding me demanded it. My pussy clenched, wet for him from that single word alone. Yet he wouldn't give me his name. An admirer. No one admired me from near or far. There was nothing to admire about me. I was a basket case with more issues than any sane man would stick around to deal with.

Without hesitation, I gave him my name even as I mentally slapped a palm to my face. I hadn't meant to, but it was out of my mouth without a thought out of habit.

I could feel his erection pressing against my ass, but he didn't try to grind it on me. I don't even know that he realized we were pressed that firmly together that I could feel it.

A nip to my ear had a gasp escaping my lungs as he gave me instructions to return to him. Then he was gone.

Spinning around, I expected to find that he'd just stepped back from me, but instead he'd completely vanished into thin air.

Breathing hard, I leaned against the wall where he'd been only moments ago. My clit was throbbing worse than it had before I'd slipped into the bathroom. Although I only knew him as Master J, everything about the quick exchange had my blood hot and desperate again.

Before I could even get a good rhythm going, I heard heels on the floor. Tugging my dress down, I shook my head at my behavior. I had to escape before I got caught and really embarrassed myself.

Upon returning to Jennifer, I stared at my hands — my mind battling what my decision would be. Could I say yes? Could I come back? Would it be a step forward or backwards in the crazy whirlwind of addiction I constantly lived in? Did it have anything to do with that?

Finally, I couldn't take the sounds of leather or skin slapping skin that filled the room. I caught Jennifer's wide eyes and motioned at the door and she rapidly nodded. I think she'd most definitely gotten more than she bargained for by coming to the club. Meanwhile, I'd been invited back by a man I hadn't seen and knew nothing about except that the barest brush of his lips on my neck had turned my body to mush and he held me like he had every right to do it. In everything I'd been through, I'd never reacted so violently to someone so quickly — or ever.

Jennifer dropped me off at the hotel so I could pick up my car. The entire drive she'd tried to talk about what we'd just seen, but was unable to complete even one sentence. I giggled at her. Obviously, her mind had been blown.

That night I lay in bed, unable to get even a wink of sleep because I couldn't get all the glorious scenes out of my head. His voice haunted me, replaying over and over. It was so incredibly sexy with that slight British accent as he handled me like he knew my body better than even I did.

When my alarm went off in the morning, I groggily rolled out of bed and proceeded to get ready for the day. I was exhausted, but I hoped a few cups of coffee would help remedy that. Thankfully, Jennifer wasn't at work so I didn't have to worry about her peppering me with questions and wanting my opinion on everything after she'd had a night to gather her thoughts. The woman spoke so quickly, I could only imagine what she'd be like after the way her eyes practically popped out of her head at the party.

Unfortunately I didn't have any appointments until the afternoon, so my mind had all that free time to continue tossing about my options and reasons for each. To the outside observer I was doing paperwork and checking on shipments and deliveries needed for parties that were coming up, but my insides were much busier.

After a couple of hours passed and I was still unable to focus on anything productive, I gave in and put my information into an online counseling site I'd found that had great reviews. I really didn't want to have to go in person to talk to someone about my problems flaring up again. It was embarrassing enough the first time, let alone to admit that I had fallen yet again.

The doctor didn't seem all that helpful, and when he suggested I come into the office to meet him in person, I quickly disengaged. I couldn't handle that on top of everything. I'd have to try again when I was at home, when I hopefully wouldn't be as jumpy. It'd been stupid to even talk to the doctor while at work. I needed to get my mind off my problems, not focus on them more than I already was.

Once appointments started showing up, the rest of the day flew by and I found myself pacing my living room, still debating. Master J had said that I was to show up at the same time as the day before. Was that the time that we had arrived or the time that he was talking to me? I hadn't paid attention to exactly when we'd arrived or when he'd caught me in the hallway. Hell, I guess I'd already made up my mind that I was going. It was a matter of what time. Would it matter? I didn't know. Didn't want to find out.

I had to find out if my reaction to him was a one-time thing or if it would happen again. It didn't help that I also wanted to put a face to the voice that still caused me to break out into shivers when I thought of it.

Not giving myself a chance to back out, I changed into a pair of black pants and a silk blouse; I wore both to work, but it was the best I had that worked for dressy casual. Leaving my hair in the low ponytail I'd worn all day, I grabbed my purse and headed to the club.

Wiping a sweaty palm on my pants, I opened the car door once I'd parked in front of the building from the night before. It looked exactly the same. Some part of me thought things would look different, but nothing had changed. Taking a deep breath, I exited the car and walked swiftly to the door of the building.

The single man standing guard by the door lifted an eyebrow at me when I stopped in front of him. He nodded over his shoulder for me to go in. Swallowing hard, I stepped past him.

Once inside, I was greeted by a new woman waiting to take my belongings. Before she could speak, I held out my purse and said, "I'm here for Master J."

"Ah. Yes." She smiled briefly before pulling back the curtain for me.

Looking from her to the curtain, I wasn't certain what I was expected to do. Would he find me once I was inside? Was I to wait for someone to come get me? When she didn't say anything else, I stepped through the curtain to find the same massive room, still clogged with people like the night before. People milling about, whipping, spanking, consensual torture — like it hadn't been nearly twenty-four hours since I'd left.

"Please follow me," a man in a black shirt and pants said before walking off, not waiting to see if I was following.

After a moment's hesitation, I quickly caught up to him. Nerves kept any of the half-naked people or arousing sounds from affecting me. I was much too focused on what I was about to walk into to even think about watching. When my escort opened a door and gestured for me to enter, I blew out a breath and did as I was told. Finding myself in a small room with another door directly in front of me, I spun around.

"Your instructions are there." He pointed to a small table behind the door he still held partially open, then quietly closed the door, leaving me in the small space.

Immediately I picked up the paper to read what was left for me.

> *Precious,*
> *Strip then kneel in the center of the room with your head down, hands on your knees. Do not speak. Do not waste time. Simply follow my instructions and you will be rewarded. Don't and you will be punished.*
> *Time is of the essence.*
> *Master J*

I read the note four times before I finally comprehended that he expected me to get naked for him. I couldn't do that. I didn't even know what he looked like. I didn't even know his name or what he wanted to do with me. I was only going to do part of what he wanted; I highly doubted he would punish me on the first time I met him. I dropped the note on the table again before kicking off my shoes, then walked through the door I hadn't been through yet. On the other side was an expansive room. It contained a large bed along with a bench of some sort and chains on one wall. Another wall was covered with hooks displaying tools for torture. Looking at the display only filled me with dread and fear that I had made a massive mistake.

Even fearing the pain that I might encounter, I was still wildly curious. Seeing a large square mat near the door, I hoped that was where I was meant to kneel. It looked much softer than the floor would have been. Dropping down, I rested my butt on my feet, hands on my thighs and looked toward the ground as instructed. Only I was still fully clothed. I refused to get naked for a man I didn't even know.

As if I had been watched, a door on the opposite side of the room opened shortly after I got settled. Breathing deeply, I caught his scent. That unique smell that was dark and earthy and unlike anything else I'd ever smelled wrapped around me making me close my eyes in pleasure. When I opened them again, there was a pair of glossy dress shoes directly in front of me. I hadn't heard him move and jumped at the unexpected sight.

"Precious, do you have problems following instructions?" The voice I'd dreamed about was exactly as I'd remembered sending a shiver of excitement down my spine.

"No, sir," I murmured in response.

"Then tell me, why are you still fully clothed?" His shoes disappeared from my view and I started to turn my head to follow, but he snapped out harshly, "I didn't tell you to move."

Immediately, I dropped my eyes to the floor again. Hearing the authority in his voice made me want to squeeze my thighs together; my pussy clenched.

"Good girl." He patted me on the head, letting me know that he was standing behind me. "You may now look up. And I am still waiting for an answer."

Lifting my head, I fought the temptation to turn and look at him. A black silk cloth was dropped in front of my face. I knew what it was and it made me straighten my back a bit more. "Sir, why am I being blindfolded? I would like to look at you since I have yet to see your face."

"And *I* would like to know why you felt the need to disobey my orders." The soft cloth was brought to my face and deftly tied behind my head, completely blocking my sight.

"I thought it was inappropriate to be naked with a man I had only met once," I calmly answered.

"I will not cause you to come by any harm that is unwanted." I heard the soft swish of his slacks as he moved around me.

Any harm that is unwanted. That part kept repeating in my head. Swallowing hard, I wiped my dewy palms on my pants again. "I don't want any harm done to me."

"Have you already forgotten the first thing I told you to remember?" He said in a husky tone near my ear.

"No, sir. I'm sorry. I'm just overwhelmed, sir." Again I felt a soft pat on the head.

"We will take it one step at a time, Precious. I will prepare you for each and everything that is going to be done to you before hand. There will be no unexpected surprises. You need to trust me. The more you trust me, the more enjoyable it will be." His voice came from directly in front of me.

"I don't know you. Why should I trust you?" Again, I felt like I should have thought my actions through more, but curiosity made me want to see where things were going.

"You shouldn't." The tone of his voice sent a chill down my back.

Chapter 6

John

Alix asked all the right questions, although she'd put herself in danger's path by meeting up with an unknown man, alone in a room with him. She was also feeling me out and testing me.

Smiling, I lifted her chin with a knuckle. "I will earn your trust. If you will let me, that is."

It took her a moment before she licked her lips and nodded.

"Good girl." I stepped back from her and folded my arms over my chest. "Tell me. What is it that you desire? What are you absolutely not willing to do?"

"I'm not sure, sir. I've never done anything like I saw people doing in the big room." Her voice was soft, unsure.

"I'm going to list things. You tell me yes or no or if you are curious to find out." Clearing my throat, I started with the most simple things and what she may have had experience with. "Spanking?"

"Yes."

"With paddles?"

"Yes."

"Floggers?"

"Yes."

"Spanking by hand?"

"Yes." She let out a lusty sigh.

"Spanking with a belt?"

"Maybe."

"Whip?"

"No. I don't think I could handle that."

"Okay. How about a crop?"

"Yes. Oh yes," she purred with a dreamy smile.

"Bondage?"

"Yes." She smiled as she replied.

"Clamps?"

"Maybe?" Her voice wavered.

"Clothespins a maybe as well?"

"Yes, sir. I'm willing to try it."

"Gags?"

"Maybe."

"Humiliation?"

"No."

"Noted. Wax play?"

"Maybe. I've wanted to try it, but it scares me."

"Nothing to be afraid of, Precious. How about piercing play?"

"No. Absolutely not."

"Fisting?"

"Maybe."

"Anal play?"

"Um... Yes?"

"We will explore it. Temperature play?"

"Yes."

"Almost done. Violet Wand?"

"I don't know what that is, sir."

"Electrical play?"

"No. Please, no."

"Sense play?"

"Possibly."

"We will start small and go from there, based on your reactions." As eager as I was to get my hands on her body, I had to know her limits. That alone would help me earn her trust and not surprise her. "First, though, tell me what made you come back?"

"You, sir. The way you touched me like you knew me. Your hands knew my body even though they've never touched it. Your voice had me panting with just a few whispered words. I had to know if it was a fluke or if it was you." Her voice was confident and strong.

Yanking on her hair tie, I released her hair from the horrendous ponytail. I fisted my hand in the free-flowing locks, pulling her head back. "Don't wear your hair pulled back unless I tell you to. Ever," I purred into her ear.

"Sorry, sir," she moaned, breathing fast.

"You'll learn how to please me, Precious. Just as you'll learn I'll pleasure you unlike you've ever had before." I knew I would be able to. The woman quickly fell into a submissive role when she'd never submitted before. She liked all of the things I liked to do to my subs. Yes, we would get a long quite well. Releasing her hair, I stepped back. "Stand. Head down. Shoulders back."

Slowly, she stood and followed my orders.

"If you can't take what I'm doing, you can say your safe word. The word you can say to make everything stop is *edge*. Do you understand? It tells me you are on the edge and can't take any more. I will immediately stop when you say this word. Repeat the word to me." I stared at her beautiful face from only inches away. The best idea I'd ever come up with had been to blindfold her. I could get as close as I wanted without worrying she'd see me. I didn't want her to know who I was. I wanted to have this single thing as my own secret. My own jewel to enjoy. I didn't want the questions that would come from her seeing me at the hotel, and my job, which always wore on every relationship I had. It had been too long since I had a submissive and something about this woman made it impossible for me to deny what I was any longer.

"Edge." Her soft, feminine voice made the word seem so much sexier than it should have.

"Good. Don't forget it." Placing both my hands on her shoulders, I dragged them slowly down her arms until I gripped a wrist in each hand. "I am going to restrain you now."

When she didn't respond, I nipped her ear, earning myself another moan from her.

"You must respond when I ask you a question," I demanded.

"Yes, sir," she whispered.

"Now, tell me, are you okay with restraints?"

"Yes, sir." She nodded her head in agreement as well.

Pulling both wrists behind her back, I wrapped them with a silk ribbon from my pocket just like the one over her eyes. Once finished, I tugged on the knot to show her how loose the ribbon was. Grabbing a pair of scissors from the wall, I walked in front of her. "You see, there is a reason why I asked you not to be wearing clothes. Naked would've been best, but panties would've worked as well. Since you didn't follow instructions, I'm going to have to do it for you, which doesn't make me too happy."

"Sorry, sir."

Even though it was the first time we were together, she needed to learn the way of things right away. Dragging the tip of the scissors from her collar bone to the dip in her top, I gave her a hint of what was coming. "Your top is not going to be wearable home. I have one that you can wear instead."

"Okay." Chewing on her bottom lip, she let her nerves show.

Slowly, I slid the scissors down the center of her top, revealing inch by inch of her flawless skin. My cock jumped, desire soaring through me at the sight. A couple of quick snips and the fabric floated to the ground around her ankles. A see-through, white lace bra was all that kept her breasts from me. Licking my lips, I forced myself to put the scissors down and picked up a crop with a hard tip.

"Stand very still. We'll see if you can tell me what this is." Deliberately sliding the tip along her spine, I smiled as goosebumps appeared on her skin.

"That is a crop, sir." Her voice took on a husky tone telling me she more than liked the crop as I had suspected.

"Very good." Trailing the hard leather over her shoulder, I stepped around her to follow the swell of her breasts. A quick, soft slap to the exposed skin of each earned me a soft moan. Alix arched her back, pressing her breasts toward me, begging for more with her luscious body. Ignoring her silent plea, I unleashed a dozen more soft, teasing pats with the crop upon her stomach, side and upper arms.

"More, sir. Harder," Alix moaned, again thrusting her breasts toward me.

I had let the first time slide, but I couldn't allow her to continue attempting to control the situation. Dropping the crop, I fisted a hand in her hair, grabbing a handful of her hip in the other, pulling her firmly against my body. My grip wasn't careful or tender; it was harsh and hard — reprimanding. "Trust me to know what you need. You will not speak unless I ask you what you want. There is a reason for going slowly and you need to allow me to show you."

"Sorry, sir. I was just trying to help." She rotated her hips against my throbbing cock.

"There will be no sex, either." I knew she wasn't ready for that experience and I wasn't ready to let her take that step, not if I wanted to have her trained properly.

"Why not, sir? I can tell you are more than ready, as am I." Again she rotated her hips.

Grinding my hips against the surge in pleasure, I released her before grabbing the ribbon around her wrists. With a little pressure, I directed her to where I wanted her. "Bend over, naughty girl." Pressing a firm hand to her upper back, I made her press her chest to the bed while still standing. "You will get five spankings with my hand. You will count them loudly or I will add more. Do you understand?"

"Yes, sir. I can take it, sir." She pressed her forehead to the mattress, instead of turning it to the side like I expected.

The dress pants she had on made her ass look especially nice when she was bent over the bed. Firmly rubbing my hand along each plump cheek, I gave her time to anticipate when the first one was coming. After a moment, I landed a palm solidly against her ass.

Without hesitation, Alix shouted, "One, sir."

The next one came down on the opposite side and again she counted without a grunt, groan, moan or cry. She'd been spanked before, that much was instantly obvious. Sliding a hand up her spine, I pulled her head back by her hair, which earned me a moan. "Can you take more than my hand?"

"Yes, sir. Please, sir." Sucking her plump bottom lip into her mouth, she smiled.

Releasing her hair, I retrieved the dropped crop and returned to her. Carefully, I slapped her back with it, letting her know what was coming. "Start at three."

"Yes, sir." Again, her forehead was to the mattress and her fingers, still tied behind her back were completely relaxed.

Not using too much strength, I landed a slap to one ass cheek with the hard tip of the crop. No reaction again, except the number. Putting a little more behind the next one, I landed the fourth one to the opposite cheek.

"Mmm. Four, sir." She turned her head to the side on the mattress, a large smile on her face.

"Better, right?" I licked my lips as she did the same.

"Much," she murmured, the smile never leaving her face.

Finally, I had a baseline on how much pain she could take without it bothering her. Not that the last one seemed to bother her, but it got a reaction none-the-less. The last blow was the hardest one and she counted for me with another moan and smile to go with it.

"Did you enjoy that?" I asked, rubbing a hand over her ass lightly.

"Yes, sir. I've had much worse spankings," she said, confirming my thoughts.

"Stand," I ordered as I tugged on the ribbon around her wrists. Once she was standing I instructed her to lie on the bed while I went to the light switch. As soon as she was situated, I flipped off the lights and went to the opposite side of the bed. Climbing on, I stayed on my knees. "Now comes the aftercare. Every time you come to me, we will have time set aside for me to care for you and make sure everything is okay. All right?"

"Yes, sir." Her voice smiled even in the dark.

"You may remove the blindfold if you'd like. I doubt you are used to being without your sight for so long." I knew it was risky, but it was dark enough she wouldn't be able to see my face. Sitting with my back against the headboard, I pulled her over onto me, her head resting on my chest.

"Would you remove it for me, sir? You are the one that put it on." Her palm slid up my chest, wrapping around the side of my neck as she tilted her head up as if she were looking at my face.

I'd never met a woman so naturally submissive. She picked up and exhibited every mannerism a trained submissive would. Reaching behind her head, I pulled the ribbon off for her.

As soon as the blindfold was off her, her lips were on mine. She straddled my waist, pressing into me. "Please, sir, fuck me. I need it. Everything you've done to me has only turned me on to the point that it is painful. I need release, sir."

When I felt her shift her weight so she could swoop in for another kiss, I grabbed her hair, keeping her from being able to complete her action. Running my nose up her neck, breathing her scent in, I slowly shook my head. "Not happening, naughty girl. I will let this single offense go without further punishment. This is called topping from the bottom. You are trying to make me do what you want and it will not work, Precious.

You ask if there is something you want, you do not take without permission. I'm sorry you are so turned on it is painful, but you need to learn discipline. If you ever want me to help you with that problem, you need to prove to me you are worth it. Prove you can be a good submissive who follows directions. Can you do that?"

"Yes, sir." Her voice was barely above a whisper. After a moment of silence, she swallowed audibly. "Sir, I can only promise to try."

"Why is that?" I asked, releasing her hair to let my hand glide down her back to rest on her hip.

"It's too embarrassing to talk about, sir. It's a problem for me." Her bottom lip quivered and she attempted to withdraw from me, shifting off my lap.

"I'm not going to push right now, but I do want to know. I want to know everything about you. The more I know, the stronger our relationship will be." I ran a hand over her hair, pulling her head back to my chest. "The more of a relationship we will build. That is, if you want to. If you want to come back and learn more, experience more. It's completely up to you."

"I do. I want to come back. I want to learn more about you as well, sir." She nuzzled her head into me, wrapping her arm around my waist.

"Knowing me isn't whats important. You are what is important. However, I do understand that you are curious, so each time we are together you can ask me two questions. I will answer them as best I can. My job and my name are the only two things I will not answer, at least right now. If we come to something else I don't feel you need to know, I will address it at that time." I didn't have to let her know me, but I knew it would make it easier for her to trust me if she knew more about me.

"Do I get two questions tonight?" she asked quickly, rising and looking in my direction.

I was going to have to leave because my eyes were adjusting to the darkness thanks to the slim line of light from under both doors. I could see faint outlines within the dark, which meant that she would be able to see as well, possibly even more after the darkness behind the blindfold. Not wanting to rush out on her, I agreed she could ask her two questions.

"Are you married?" was her first question. "Or have you been married in the past?"

"Is that going to be both of your questions for the night?" I reminded her of the limit. I hadn't been married before, but I was going to make her work for every bit of information.

"No," she snapped quickly then breathed deeply. "Just are you currently married?"

"No."

She sat quietly for a moment before asking her second question. "Why can't I know your name?"

Chapter 7

Alix

With each question he asked about what I was and wasn't willing to do, I breathed harder. My body temperature rose as the need for release escalated to heights I'd never felt before. When my addition had been at it's peak, I'd experimented with many positions in bed trying to find the one that felt the best, but nothing had come even close to what he made me feel. Maybe it had to do with the BDSM aspect, maybe it was simply him.

I found it easy to call him "sir" when I spoke to him. It was the tone of his voice, the manner in which he touched me. He wasn't a fumbling, lost idiot. Each touch, each caress was purposeful, thought out. However, when it came to his so-called spankings, I could tell he was holding back. I wanted him to let loose on me; I wanted to feel the harsh flick of the leather against my skin when he used the crop or hear the crack of skin meeting skin from a spanking. Why wasn't I nervous around this man who had cut off my shirt? Because he'd done everything possible to make me feel reassured and safe. Not one touch was in a groping or sexual way. Even when I'd been restrained and at my most vulnerable, he'd been calculated, calm and controlled. He could've tied my hands tightly and I wouldn't have complained, but he didn't. He made sure that I knew that I could easily get out of the restraint if I wanted to, but I didn't. I liked handing over the control to see what he could do with it.

In the end, though, I was greatly disappointed that he'd said no to sex, but that didn't stop me from going home to find release on my own. I'd tried to force the issue, but again, ever so calmly he'd told me it wasn't going to happen. I'd anticipated more punishment because I'd known I was breaking the rules by trying to get him to break his own restraint. None came, sadly.

I feared that he would restrict my release, tell me I couldn't help myself, but he hadn't and I wasn't going to bring it up. I didn't think even with his order I'd be strong enough to not do it, especially after all the yummy experiences that I had just been through.

When he said I could have two questions, I nearly jumped off the bed to do a happy dance. I didn't think it was fair for this man to want to know so much about me, but not be willing to give something of himself in return. First things first, though— I had to know if why he didn't want me to see him was because he was hiding something major, like a little wifey at home. After he said no, I debated with myself on how to phrase or even to ask the question that was on the tip of my tongue.

Finally, I knew I just had to say it. I had to at least ask. Gathering my nerves, I quickly spilled the question. "Why can't I know your name?"

"It's just a name. It's a common name at that. It doesn't define me. It doesn't tell you anything about me, really. It is just a name." He didn't hesitate with his answer, as if he'd known that I was going to ask it all along.

"Then how will I know what to call you besides

'sir'?" How would I talk about him to anyone if I didn't have a name to give him without calling him "sir"? That would only make conversations awkward. Then again, maybe that was the point of not telling me his name.

"You can call me Master or Sir. If you absolutely must, you can call me Master J. And that was a third question, but I will allow it as it is something you should know."

I could see the faintest outline of his body in the dark room. I'd felt how strong and hard his body was when I'd pressed against him. When my head had rested upon his chest, I'd felt the buttons of a dress shirt; that, along with the glimpse of his shiny shoes, told me he was dressed in business attire. Not that any of that would really make him stand out in a crowd if I were to run into him again. However, his voice, with the British accent and hard tone, most certainly would.

"Lie down," he said and I did as he instructed, curious to see where things were headed. I had thought our time was coming to a close, but would be more than happy to stay for more. A soft chuckle caressed my senses before he told me to roll onto my stomach. "Lower your pants to just below your cheeks."

Without a word, I quickly did so.

"I'm going to turn the lights up. Do you think you can control yourself and keep your eyes closed or do you need me to blindfold you?" As he spoke, I felt the bed shift as he stood.

"I will keep them closed, sir." I already had them closed so all I had to do was resist the temptation to sneak a peek.

His footsteps drifted away, only to return.

There was a dim light behind my eyelids, but I kept them closed as I felt his hands glide over my skin.

"Just checking to make sure you are okay after taking a few taps from the crop," he informed me. "You may stand and fix your pants. There is a spare shirt in the room you entered through, along with a note from me. Thank you for coming tonight."

I lay still, unsure if I was actually supposed to get up or not. When I heard the click of a door closing, I knew that I was alone again. Rolling over, I sat up. My bottom wasn't sore at all from the crop so I doubted there was much of anything for him to see, but it didn't bother me one ounce to have his hands on me. Fixing my pants, I stood then walked back through the door I had come in through. I didn't look around, didn't care. I could tell he was gone, the room felt much emptier without him in it and there was nothing else that interested me. Folded neatly where the initial note had been were a button-down shirt and another note.

Setting the note aside, I pulled the shirt on, lifting it to my nose to breathe in his scent. It smelled just like him. Smiling as I buttoned it up, I thought of how swiftly things had changed. It hadn't been so long since I'd walked into the room bound and determined to do things my way when it came to Master J. Snuggling the shirt that swallowed me, I enjoyed the comfort and security our time brought me even if I wasn't that much more informed than when I'd arrived. At least I knew what was expected when we met, not to mention I felt the flutters in my stomach that normally came with meeting someone you were intensely interested in.

Picking up the note, I slipped my shoes on and sat on the small stool to read it.

Precious,

> *I hope you enjoyed our time together as much as I did.*
> *When you are ready to submit to me again, call or text me.*
> *Master J*

Underneath his name his number was scrawled in the same masculine script as the rest of the note.

The ball was in my court, so to speak. The man continued to surprise me. Even with as dominant as he was, he left the option and decision up to me. It was ultimately my choice to contact him again or not. After everything I'd heard about the BDSM community and how controlling and abusive it was, I was having a hard time relating it to my experiences.

Collecting myself, I let myself out; thankfully, there wasn't anyone else in the hallway and I was able to escape to my car without having to interact with anyone but the woman with my bag at the front. Once in my car I was tempted to pull out my phone and message him right away, but instead I forced myself to drive home. It was a small little house on the outskirts of town. Since I'd spent so much time at home instead of going out, I'd managed to save up a nice little stash and had only purchased it a few months prior.

Once there, I put my purse on the counter and pulled out my phone. Placing the note and my phone next to each other, I stared at the pair for a good long while as I debated on what I was going to do. Eventually, I couldn't wait any more. Picking up my phone, I tapped out a quick message and sent it before heading off to get ready for bed. I stood in my room, looking at dresser where my pajamas were stored before deciding I was going to sleep in his shirt. No one would know. It was just me and it was surprisingly comforting having his scent with me. I did, however, kick off my pants and remove my bra to be more comfortable.

Walking back to the kitchen, I picked up my phone to find I had a return message.

My initial message was on top:

> I had more fun than I expected and look forward to next time, Master.

In a gray bubble signaling his response was:

Oh to hear you call me in person. I leave our next meeting date up to you.

Smiling, I knew he'd be surprised by the use of Master as I hadn't called him that so far.

> I won't know until I double check my schedule at work.

A moment passed before his response popped up:

I'll be waiting.

Taking my phone to my room, I plugged it in and tumbled into bed. Surrounded by his scent, the memories of the night flooded my mind causing me to get turned on again.

I tried to tell myself that I could simply roll over and ignore it. I didn't have to give into the fiery hot desire throbbing through my body at the remembered sensations of Master's swats on my ass or the feel of his arms wrapped around me. The more I tried not to give in, the more my body throbbed — the ache escalating.

Rolling to my back, a hand slipped under my panties before I even had time to think about it and angrily pushed my swollen clit around. The night played out over and over in my head as I continued to circle and bang against my clit. Even after twenty minutes of focusing on it, I couldn't reach the peak I was craving. Sighing, I rolled over and threw open my drawer filled with toys. It only took a second to find my favorite vibrator. It slid right into my needy pussy when I pushed against my opening. Cranking up the vibrations, I returned to teasing my clit as I slid the thick toy in and out.

The longer it took, the angrier I got, but once I started it was impossible to convince myself to stop until I finally got off. After another fifteen minutes, I finally felt the beginnings of an orgasm building. Unfortunately, the small cresting wave that I caught wasn't all that fulfilling, but it would have to do because I was exhausted. Even so, I tossed and turned for hours with Master's voice and actions rolling around in my head, keeping my body at a simmer.

During the middle of the night I couldn't take it any longer and slipped my hand between my thighs to once more try to get off. Anything to release some of the tension that was keeping me from getting a good night's sleep. Yet again, my body refused to give me what I wanted and I was more rough than I had intended, leaving myself sore, tired, sweaty and still barely satiated.

Hours later my alarm jolted me awake. Even after silencing the annoying thing, it took me a few minutes to get out of the bed and start my daily ritual of getting ready for work. Since I was sore between my legs from the rough night, I put on a loose skirt, thigh highs and heels — no panties. They'd just rub and make things worse. Plus it was Sunday, and sexy, mystery man didn't show up on Sundays so ideally my pussy and hormones would behave for a few hours at least.

I did have an event to deal with where I would be standing and walking quite a bit, so I slipped a pair into my purse just in case things got sweaty. My life was practical, not sexy, sadly.

Once I blow-dried my hair and curled it, I pulled on another silk top not much different from the one I'd worn the night before. As flashes of the evening swamped me, I quickly whipped it off and put on a button-up top. Again it made me think of Master J, but I ran out of time and if I wasted any more I'd be late for work.

Grabbing my purse and keys, I ran out the front door. As I pulled into my parking spot at the hotel, I realized with a hot flash of horror that I'd forgotten my phone at home. One more reason I would have to behave while at work, even though I would have much rather have been able to text him as soon as I double-checked my calendar for upcoming events. I couldn't wait to meet up with him again even if I didn't get sexual gratification from it; the feelings it gave mel to let him have control of me gave me a rush while at the same time created a calm, quiet place my mind already craved.

Walking in the front door of the hotel, I saw Jennifer was in so it was going to be a busy day of gossip if she got her way. I already had a busy event to deal with so I was hoping I might be able to put it off for another day. Only time would tell.

Chapter 8

John

I was glad I'd already arranged to have the shirt out of my bag and a note left for Alix after I left her. I'd had to force myself to leave the room before I snapped and fucked her raw. She wanted it, she was begging me to do it, but she wasn't ready. I wanted more from our relationship than a quick fuck.

Even as my dominant side pushed for me to take over everything in her life, I knew I had to let it be her choice where this thing was going. I already had quite a bit of control over things and didn't want to make her run by taking too much from her. That's not the type of dom I was. I refuse to force a woman to do things she doesn't want to do, including spending time with me.

When a woman truly submits and hands over their control to you, that's when it's exhilarating. When the choice is there and they choose you, they choose to submit of their own free will when they could just as easily not.

I was disciplined and in control of myself enough to let her take the choice of when we would meet. Once she was in my grasp again, I would take over.

After spending hours working with patients online, I looked at my phone again. Alix was supposed to send me her schedule. She didn't say exactly when she got it, but I expected it in the morning hours. By one, I grumbled in irritation. I wanted to text her, but it was her turn.

Grabbing my wallet and keys off the counter, I took the elevator down to the lobby of the hotel. I knew she'd be down there. Since she didn't know what I looked like, I could easily get a glimpse of her then return to my computer. Another plus of her not knowing who I was. I could see her as much as I wanted and she'd never know. If she knew, she might think it a bit stalker-ish.

Laughing at that thought, I knew it was just another side of my dom coming out. The need to know where my woman was.

In the lobby, I glanced toward her office, but it was empty. That meant she was probably near or in the ballroom with an event of some kind. I debated for a moment on how I would be able to excuse being in that area, then I figured, who cared? Hotel guests always went where they weren't supposed to.

I knew where all the event rooms were; I'd even attended functions in many of them over the years. I'd never had the pleasure of meeting the woman behind them, though. She was always a fixture around the outside of the event, making sure everything was going as planned. Without her knowledge, I'd been watching her for far longer than I'd ever admit to anyone. Then one day she'd caught me watching her and it became a game of who could sneak glimpses without being noticed.

My body caught fire when her eyes were on it. I didn't have to look at her to know when she was watching me; I felt it. After months and months of playing the little game we played, she appeared in that club. My control snapped and I grabbed her while I could. It was my one and only chance to finally get what

I wanted.

Following sounds of laugher and the dull hum of chatter, I found the room where the event was. It was packed and most people were wearing semi-formal or business attire. I was in a pair of jeans and a plain shirt; I wouldn't be able to join the party without standing out.

Damn.

Shoving my hands in my pockets out of frustration, I turned around to head back to my suite. To my surprise, I nearly bowled over Jennifer and Alix. While Alix gave me a shy smile and ducked her head, Jennifer's hands grabbed my biceps as she purred.

"I'd say sorry, John, but really I'm not since I caught myself on these hunky arms." Jennifer smiled at me. I nodded my head and stepped to the side, letting her arms drop. Alix threw a glare at her before looking away again. Sighing, Jennifer continued, "I thought you'd have heard us coming up behind you. We were discussing Alix's wild night."

I lifted an eyebrow at her as a smirk came over my face. I found it hard to believe that Alix would have spilled much about our time together to a gossiper like Jennifer, but I didn't have to respond.

Gasping, Alix slapped Jennifer's arm before stalking into the party. shaking her head.

"She's so easy to upset. She wouldn't even tell me any details, just that she had a date — like it was such a big deal to have a date." Jennifer ran her fingers through her hair.

"Maybe it is for her. Not everyone lives the life you do. And not everyone feels the need to share all their personal business," I informed her, feeling like I needed to stand up to the woman if Alix wasn't going to.

"John, she totally knows I'm kidding. The girl is entirely too shy and quiet for her own good. I'm just trying to get her to open up and have some fun." Jennifer rolled her eyes at me. "You know, like the kind I could show you."

"No, doll. You can't show me anything, but thank you for the offer." I started to walk down the hall away from her.

"The offer is always open if you change your mind." She raised her voice enough to make sure I heard her.

Not giving her any reaction, I continued walking. She needed someone to take her over their knee and give her a good paddling for that mouth of hers, but I had my eye on Alix.

Upon returning to my room, I still didn't have any messages on my phone. It wasn't until hours later when I was getting ready to meet a client at their house that I finally got a text message from her.

> I'm so sorry I didn't get back to you earlier, but I forgot my phone at home. Can we meet Wednesday or would the weekend work better for you?

Weekdays worked better for me since my clients normally liked for me to meet with then on the weekends. Although I did have a few that liked meeting during the week — with their mistresses.

Wednesday works perfectly. Seven at the club?

That works. See you there.

I didn't have to look at my calendar. I would move any appointments I had if they interfered. Meeting up with Alix was more important than helping any of my clients out. My cock lengthened and throbbed just from the thought of getting my hands on Alix again. But I didn't have time to dwell on the delicious things I had planned for her; I had to get to my appointment.

Since it was a Monday, I was meeting with clients at their home. Steven and Julie had been patients of mine for quite a while. They'd used me to open the door to numerous avenues they wouldn't normally have felt comfortable talking about or bringing up with each other. They wanted to do a threesome, but it was quite the task to find a willing third. Until we did, we explored other play options.

Parking my Mercedez in front of their house, I pulled the door down to close it. Just closing the door made me smile and glee shoot through me. One of my favorite purchases I'd ever made. Fast, sleek, and sexy as hell. The gull-wing doors that opened up instead of out like most cars were what had sunk me when I was looking to upgrade my car a few months prior. Not to mention that, although not cheap, it was nowhere near as expensive as the other cars I had my eye on.

The front door of the large house opened as soon as I started up the driveway. Julie strutted down the path toward me, meeting me halfway.

"Good evening, sir." Julie ran her hands over her voluptuous hips as she licked her lips.

"Hello, Julie." I was used to her antics. She was all bark, no bite. She was a harmless flirt, but she'd never attempted to take it any farther than that whether her husband was around or not. Wrapping an arm around her shoulders, I steered her back toward the house. "How are you this evening?"

"Better now that you're here." Her arm looped

around my waist, pausing along the way to squeeze my ass.

Flicking my eyes at her, I gave her a warning glare. I'd let her get away with it once and she knew it.

Once in the house, she led me to the master bedroom and softly shut the door behind us. She'd filled the silence with mindless chatter about how she'd been looking forward to our appointment and her husband was as well. He was waiting for me in a spare room across the hall from the master, as was our usual practice. I would prep Julie, then give her time to get ready before giving Steven his pointers and tips for the evening.

It was unusual that a couple required my services as long as this one had. Normally after learning how to open the lines of communication about things in the bedroom, it became easier for the couple to do so without needing an intermediary, such as myself. Some couples didn't. Julie and Steven were the perfect example of that. No matter how many unusual items either of them had me help introduce, they still required that assistance in bringing it up with their partner without fear of rejection or judgment. Sometimes it was simply that they liked the feeling of being exhibitionists, since there was another person in the room.

"Sit on the side of the bed, Julie. Let's get started so Steven isn't waiting long," I instructed her, letting my dom voice come out.

A shiver rolled through her plump body as she stepped up to the bed. Her lust-filled eyes rolled over me. "Ooh, you know I like when you talk to me like that. All British and sexy like."

"My voice is always British," I laughed, walking

closer to her.

"Mmm, but when you get all demanding and controlling it's more so. It's thicker and sexy as hell," Julie moaned, sliding a hand between her thighs.

"Julie. I am only going to say this one time… You already know that's not what I'm here for and I will refuse to help you and your husband again if it continues." I crossed my arms over my chest, disappointment clear.

"I'm sorry. I don't know what's come over me today. I think it's 'cause I'm so excited to get started." She visibly shook herself.

"Then tell me, what is it we are going to be exploring today?" I dropped my arms and let the tension release from my shoulders. I didn't like having to put my customers in an awkward position, but on the other hand, I wasn't willing to let them treat me like a piece of meat or put me in the middle of the problems in their relationship I was there to fix. If they wanted to step outside of their marriage to find whatever was missing in their relationship, they would have to look elsewhere for that.

"I'd like to fuck my husband," Julie said as an unusual smirk crept onto her face.

"Care to expand?" That was a given, since that was generally why I was brought into relationships and bedrooms.

"I want to put on a strap-on and fuck him. Or is it called pegging? Whatever. I want to give it to him. I know he wants it." Julie pulled a strap-on set-up out of a drawer near the bedside.

I nodded. It was not an unusual request from either side. "Let me talk to your husband, and then I'll come back and let you know how it goes."

She gave me an enthusiastic thumbs-up while fiddling with the straps — trying to figure out how to get it on.

Taking a calming breath, I let myself into the room across the hall after a short knock.

Steven was sitting at the desk in the corner. He turned and smiled at me as he shut his lap top. "So, what are we doing today, doc?"

"I'm not sure how comfortable you'll be with it. However, your wife seems to think you are more than ready for this step," I told him, leaning back against the door.

"Hit me with it." Pushing in the chair to the desk, Steven stood and tucked his hands in his pockets.

"She'd like to use a strap-on — on you." I waited. I'd seen just about every reaction before so I waited for his.

"I'm listening. I don't want to say that I'm excited, but I'm not completely put off by the idea either." He shrugged. "I suppose what I mean is, I'll try it. Why not? I can always change my mind, right?"

"Exactly. Try everything once is my motto." I laughed softly. "Let me go help get your wife ready and then we will have you come in."

He nodded and I made my way back to Julie. She had already figured out how to get the thick, black straps on and had a wide, hard, rubber penis hanging in front of her thighs.

"Looks sexy, right? I think so anyway. I bet he will too." Julie bit her lip in obvious excitement as she let her hand slide up and down the appendage.

"Can you wait in the bathroom just for a moment while I get Steven in here and ready?" I asked, but turned my back without waiting for an answer.

Across the hall, Steven had already shed his shirt and jeans and was waiting in only his white briefs. Again, not my favorite sight, but I'd seen worse. Quickly ushering him across the hall and onto the bed, I had him relaxed against the pillow just as Julie opened the door and sauntered into the room with nothing on but the strap-on.

"Oh wow. Jumping right in." Steven took a couple of deep breaths before nodding at his wife. "Let's do this, baby."

"It would actually be better if you exchanged some foreplay first — you know, get the motors revving and ready before you jump right into that. It'll help make it easier and less painful." I stepped up to the bed just as Julie climbed on the other side to lounge next to her husband.

"It's going to hurt?" Steven's head snapped up to look at me.

"A bit. The more foreplay and lube used, the less it'll hurt. It will feel uncomfortable until you get used to it." I reassured him.

"Have you done it?" he asked.

My least favorite question. While I would help with just about any situation my clients had, I didn't like including my personal experiences and preferences.

Smiling, I gave a one-shoulder shrug. "I don't like to share my personal stuff. Sorry." I had experienced being fucked by a woman and a man and it was pleasurable both times, but it was completely none of their business. "Just know that any time you want to stop, just say the word. Talk it out with your wife. Breathe through any discomfort. I am here to make sure everything goes smoothly so be as free and open as you can. And you can be as vocal as you'd like, it won't bother me."

"Yes, of course doc." Steven nodded rapidly.

I stepped back from the bed and let them get started kissing and fondling. Although my eyes never left the bed, my mind wandered to Alix and what it would be like to get my dick in her. I wondered if she'd ever had it up the ass or if she'd let me show her the ways of that if she hadn't.

Moaning from the couple in front of me snapped me out of my musings. Both looked to be ready to move to the fun part. They had even removed Steven's briefs while I was lost in thought. Quietly pulling on rubber gloves as protection, I stepped up next to the bed with a bottle of lube from the nightstand.

"You ready?" I quietly asked, leaning my hip against the bed to get their attention.

"Yes, God, yes," Julie mewled as she rutted the rubber penis against her husband's dark pink, dripping one.

They had already gotten themselves situated with Julie on top of Steven so I popped open the top of the container. "Let's get you all lubed up, Julie."

She sat back on her haunches and thrust the penis at me. I held the bottle clear of the appendage and let a few drops fall on it. When she continued to stare at me, expecting me to do more, I shook my head and dripped a bit more on it.

"You smooth it in. Get it ready for Steven," I told her. As she took her penis in hand and stroked it, I looked to Steven. "Spread your thighs as far as you comfortably can."

He cleared his throat uncomfortably, but did as I

asked. I let a few drops of the lube drip down the path between his balls and puckered hole. Before I could say anything else, Julie was there, rubbing it in and slowly pressing the tip of one of her fingers past the squeezing muscle.

"I know how to do this part. He likes it when I play with his ass. Don't you baby?" She confidently slid her finger in farther and farther before picking up a slow rhythm of press and slide.

"Excellent. Now gently add another finger. Keep the same rhythm." I told her. Slowly I talked her through adding another finger then changing her fingers out for the slicked-up dildo attached to her hips. Her large hips and rounded belly made it hard for her to get the angle right for the dildo though, which is what I had suspected was going to happen. Steven wasn't in any better position to help, so I reached forward and helped her line up with his tight rosette until she managed to get the head to enter him.

As soon as I could, I got my hand out from between their bodies and stepped back from the bed. They didn't need much guidance from that point so I removed my gloves and stood back to wait until they finished. It was rare that I had to "help" in that manner, and for that I was thankful. While I didn't mind watching and instructing, I didn't find pleasure in being an assistant to another like that. It made the dominant side of me want to come out and take over the situation when it wasn't my place.

I did have to help one final time when I instructed Julie to jerk her husband off while she was thrusting into his ass. Once she did that, they were both spent minutes later. After making sure the dildo was safely extracted and there wasn't any bleeding from

Steven that I could see, I left the satiated couple to enjoy their afterglow.

Chapter 9

Alix

It seemed like every second lasted minutes as the days passed, but finally it was Wednesday and I would be seeing Master J again. To say I was looking forward to it was an understatement of epic proportions. Besides, I hadn't seen John — yes, I finally had his name — since the incredibly awkward run in on Monday when I'd been with Jennifer.

She had cornered me so we could compare notes about the party. It had taken a lot not to tell her that I'd been back for a one-on-one session, but I knew she'd never leave me alone if I let that tasty little tidbit get out. I had mistakenly said that I was anxious to get home so that I could text someone. She wouldn't let me go until I'd finally admitted it was a man whom I'd had a date with the night before. She'd been in the process of trying to pry more details out of me when we'd stumbled upon John in the hallway outside of my event.

He hadn't uttered one word, but his eyes spoke volumes and his body was just as potent up-close. He'd practically ignored Jennifer until she started trying to get her greedy little claws into him. Jealousy had sparked within me at that; then again, I'd never really said a word to the man so he wasn't even close to being mine and I had no grounds for the feeling.

She'd stood in the hallway after I rushed away in an embarrassed mess. I think she tried to embarrass me on purpose, and really the last person in the world I wanted her to be telling about my so-called date was the man I frequently dreamed about. Although ever since Saturday night with Master J, my dreams had been split between that nameless, faceless man and the sexy man I'd been watching for months.

It was my turn to try to pry information out of Jennifer. I wanted to know everything she knew about John. I'd about fainted when she'd said his name. She had known his name all along and I'd finally learned it. I had a name to call out as my orgasm rushed over me at night in bed, in my shower in the morning or in the afternoon during my lunch break.

My addiction was getting out of control, I knew it. Every day I was sucked further into it's grip no matter how much I tried to fight it. I was tempted to get back online and try to talk to someone there, but I'd been too busy to make time to tear open the closet filled with skeletons. I vowed that on my next day off I would make the time. I'd set everything aside and talk to someone even if it made me uncomfortable. However, that wasn't always so easy, seeing as I was a salaried employee for the hotel. I often worked after-hours at events or I'd have to come back hours later for a function. A full day off was rare. When I did actually get one, I had so much stuff left to do that I'd barely stop all day trying to get caught up.

When my normal office hours were over, I all too happily gathered my purse and threw a wave to Jennifer before quickly making my way to my car. I didn't have time to mess around. Speeding a bit, I rushed to get home so I could shower, do my hair, shave, and dress in clean stockings, garter belt and another pair of my favorite lacy panty-bra sets. Standing in just my undergarments, I stared down my closet. I didn't have much in there that fell under "sexy" but I wanted to look good for Master J — not that he would see me fully dressed. Thankfully I had a slight addiction to fancy panties and sexy underthings. I suppose that only fed my sex addiction, but I wanted to feel pretty even if I was the only one who would see them.

Finally, I selected a button-up blouse and a knee-length skirt. That was another thing that I needed to make time for. Shopping for sexier, non-work clothes. Slipping on my four-inch heels, I grabbed my purse and sent a quick text to Master J letting him know I was coming to him.

At the club, I was greeted by a woman at the desk; she looked familiar, but I couldn't say if she was the same one as either of my previous visits or not. I was again escorted to the room I was to enter and let into a small dressing room. There was no note awaiting me, so I stripped off my skirt and blouse before stepping through the door.

Remembering my instructions from the first time, I kneeled in the middle of the room with my head down. And just like the first time, moments after I was settled, he joined me.

"Mmm, Precious, how fast you learn." Master J's British accent washed over me, causing me to shiver in pleasure.

"Yes, sir," I responded with a slight smile, keeping my head down.

"You look absolutely mouthwatering, but you, my little tease, will not get what you are begging me for." His beautiful, shiny shoes stepped into my view at the same time his unique scent washed over me.

"I'm not begging for anything, sir. I just wanted to look pretty for you," I said honestly. Not that I would complain if he wanted to go there, but he'd already said I wasn't going to be getting sex from him.

"Very well. I do not mind looking at you wearing a garter belt and hose. They are my favorite things to see on a beautiful woman. Now for the blindfold." His large hands brushed my hair back over my shoulders before tying the silky fabric over my eyes.

It didn't frighten me as it had the first time. I was ready for anything he wanted to show me.

"Stand," his deep voice demanded.

I moved to quickly comply and stood on my heels, keeping my head down.

"Fuck," he cursed under his breath but I was still able to catch it.

Tugging my lower lip between my teeth, I fought not to smile at the unintentional compliment.

"Arms up," he spoke from behind me. I hadn't heard him move and jumped at his voice coming from a different direction than expected.

After I raised up one arm and then the other, he wrapped fabric around both wrists, binding them together. It wasn't nearly as loose as it had been the first time, but still loose enough I could've probably pulled my wrists from it if I really wanted to.

"You remember your safe word?"

I nodded. "Yes. Edge."

"Good. Now walk." His large, hot hand came to rest on my lower back as he directed me. I slowly put one foot in front of the other until he told me to stop.

I could feel something close in front of me, but I wasn't sure if it was the wall or something else.

"Since you did so excellently with the crop last time, I thought we might start with something a little bit tougher than that. Okay?" he asked, surprising me.

"Yes, sir." I knew then that it must be the wall or at least something for me to lean against should I need to. I bent my arms, letting my hands fall behind my head. I didn't have anywhere else to let them go unless I wanted to completely lower my arms and I knew that wouldn't make him happy.

"Did I tell you to lower your arms?" his voice snapped at me.

My arms straightened immediately. "No, sir."

"Then why did you lower them?" he asked.

I could feel him walking behind me, back and forth, as he waited for my answer. I shrugged helplessly. "I'm not sure. I guess I figured you weren't looking and I could use the break from my burning shoulders."

"I know your shoulders are hurting. The only way to make them not hurt so quickly is to condition them. Short periods of time, which is what we are doing here. Do you really trust me so little, Precious?" His fingers brushed along my neck before dragging across the nape as he pushed all of my hair over one shoulder.

"I'm sorry, sir." I had no idea why I'd lowered them. My shoulders didn't hurt that bad. Sure, they burned a little bit, but nothing I couldn't endure for a bit longer. Hanging my head between my shoulders, I'd realized that I had been looking forward instead of down as I knew he expected of me.

"You can lift your head. Being submissive isn't about studying your shoes and letting other see your hair. You should be proud to be submissive, that you are strong enough to hand over your control to your master. Keep your shoulders up, your head up. Simply avert your eyes. Let everyone see how beautiful you are, but only I am to be graced with your eyes when I ask. Don't bow over and shy away like other submissives. That doesn't make you look any better or show that you are more submissive than the next, it only makes you look like a broken soul who is just asking for someone to stomp on you." Master J's finger hooked under my chin, raising my head back up.

"I'll try my best to remember, Master," I murmured. I was used to shying away, hiding away who I was from everyone. It would take practice for me to do as he said, but I would try.

"Now I am going to hook your arms over your head to keep them there. If you behave and are a good girl, this won't take long and your shoulders won't get too sore. If you disobey me, then we will keep starting over and it'll take longer. Understand?" As he talked, he guided the tie on my wrists up high enough that I had to lift onto my toes. When his warm hands left my wrists, I was unable to put my feet solidly on the ground, but was still supported enough to not feel like I was going to fall.

"Yes, sir." I wiggled a bit to make sure I wasn't going to fall.

"For that, you'll get a couple extra. I will see to your safety, including you accidentally falling. Trust in me." Anger was clear in his voice even as he moved farther away from me. When his footsteps returned, I swallowed hard in anticipation of what was coming.

Silence descended for longer than I was comfortable with. I wanted to say something to fill it, but knew it would only get me in more trouble as I hadn't been spoken to first. Finally, I felt something that felt like loose leather straps tracing along my back.

"We are going to try flogging tonight. Have you been flogged before?" Master J questioned even as the tickling feeling on my back continued.

"No, sir. I don't think so. It tickles. Is it supposed to tickle?" My skin jumped as it tried to get away from the sensation, completely outside of my control.

"It won't tickle once I get started. I just wanted you to know what it was that was happening." The light, teasing sensation was gone as I heard him step away from me again. However, the firm, burning one that slapped against my ass was not what I had expected to come after the tickling. After another couple of harsh, loud slaps against my ass, a different sensation started on my right shoulder blade. This time the slap against my skin came more rapidly and didn't have quite the same harsh sting to it, although it burned in a different way.

The flogger was brought down in a rapid succession, falling on one shoulder then the other before moving back to the first. The longer it went on, the more it hurt, the more intense it felt. The flogger moved all along my back before moving back up again, each stinging, burning pain harder and more intense than the one before it.

Just when I thought I would have to give in and cry out from the pain, it completely stopped.

"That was just warming you up," Master J whispered in my ear.

Again, his footsteps grew farther away before returning.

"This will be much more intense and painful. You can handle it. If you can't, you know your safe word."

Something hard and cold rubbed underneath my ass cheeks. I swallowed before responding with a quivering voice. "Yes, sir. Edge."

"Exactly. You'll be getting five of these. Four for doubting me. One because you are a little pain slut." Again the rubbing of the cold, hard, slim object, as if warning me of what was to come.

"P..pain slut?" I stuttered. I didn't know what the object was, but it made me nervous and the term he'd labeled me with didn't feel good either.

"That means you enjoy pain, Precious," he clarified.

It wasn't a question and I didn't want to expand on why pain didn't bother me. I did enjoy it, but I wasn't always that way.

"Do you know what this is?" He tapped my ass with the same object he'd been teasing me with.

"No, sir." I shuddered.

"It's a cane. It's a slim piece of bamboo. It hurts like hell. This will be the one and only time I use it unless you directly ask for it." Another soft tap on the ass.

"Yes, sir." Fear filled me, but still I tried to hold as still as I could.

"Count for me," he said, moments before a loud crack sounded and pain shot up my back and down my legs with a fire straight across my ass where the cane had landed.

"One, sir," I cried as my eyes filled with tears.
Crack.

"Two, sir," I sobbed as I fought with everything inside me to do as he asked so as not to get more punishment.
Crack.

"Three, sir." Tears flowed freely down my cheeks as my hands fisted, nails digging into my palms.

My legs threatened to give out, but I locked my knees, determined to make it through them all.

Crack.

"Four... sir." It took me a moment to get my mind to focus through a hazy cloud that was slipping over everything. My hands relaxed their grip. The fire in my ass was no longer a pain-filled burn, but a pleasure-searing flame.

Crack.

Words were out of my grasp at that moment. Nothing mattered. Nothing hurt. A calm, quiet, serene feeling filled me from head to toe and I had no desire to stop what we were doing if that meant that this blissful feeling was going to leave.

My mind hadn't been this calm in... forever. Something always needed to be done. Someone always needed something from me. The rare chance I had freedom from work, my body and the ever-nagging addiction that raged and tormented me constantly were there to keep me company and my mind busy.

Slowly, I opened my eyes, not remembering closing them. Everything was dark, no matter which way I turned. Panic swelled and I tried to jump up from wherever I was lying, but hot, strong arms tugged me tight against a warm, firm body.

"Shh. It's okay. You are okay." Soft breath brushed against the top of my head.

"Where am I? What happened?" I tried to push the spiderwebs out of my head so I could figure things out on my own.

"You went to something called subspace," Master J said as his hand brushed against the back of my hair in a soothing manner. "It's when you are pushed past pain and into pleasure. They say it's like going into a cloud. Floating and calm."

"Yeah, I suppose that's a good way to describe it." I smiled lazily. Knowing that what had happened was actually a normal reaction had me wanting to do it again.

"I'm sorry I didn't see you were already slipping before the final punishment. But I got you down as soon as I realized you'd gone nonverbal on me." That relaxing hand continued to run through and over my hair.

"Nonverbal?" I lifted an eyebrow even though he couldn't see it.

"When you are unable to respond. That can be for something feeling good or bad. Its safest to immediately stop when that happens so you don't get hurt," he explained patiently.

"Oh. Okay." I didn't know what else to say. I didn't even know such things as 'subspace' and 'nonverbal' were possibilities in such an environment.

"How are you feeling?" His voice was soft and caring. A soft thumb brushed against my cheek tenderly.

"Good. Really relaxed. I don't know if I can walk, so I hope you aren't going to tell me I have to leave right now." I laughed softly and then stopped when he didn't join me.

"No, Precious. We will stay here, just like this until you are feeling more like yourself."

A moment of uneasy quiet hung between us although I wasn't sure what it was that I'd said that bothered him.

"Can I ask my questions?" I asked, trying to bring up an easier topic.

Chapter 10

John

Walking into the room and seeing Alix on her knees with those sexy thigh-high hose and garter belt on had nearly taken my breath away. She was already heart-stopping beautiful; then to see her stripped down to barely-there panties and having her pussy so easily accessible practically broke my control. Grinding my teeth, I knew what she'd planned. She had hoped for that exact thing and she would have to take a punishment for trying to push me to fuck her when I'd already told her it wasn't happening. She swore that it hadn't been her intention and I let her think that she was going to get away with it, but she'd get her punishment for it.

When she'd stood up she showed that she'd left her heels on, which only served to elongate her legs and flex her ass as she stood there looking more perfect than any other woman I'd ever laid eyes on. I realized that she indeed had not intended to tease and push me, but didn't realize just how desirable she was. How that was even possible, I'll never know. I fought myself constantly to keep my hands from straying. Having her trained and ready to be everything I needed, while also being all that she could be, was more important than a quick romp and release.

It wasn't hard to see, ever since the first time I'd seen her in the club that she was meant for a submissive relationship. She flourished helping people; her pain tolerance was the highest I'd ever seen in a submissive. She got turned on more than hurt when the crop had landed upon her. I planned to push her further to see just how much she could take.

After hooking the ribbon around her wrists high up on the wall, I picked up a flogger, then stood admiring her submission. She was uneasy, yet she stood waiting for what I would give her after a small warning to trust in me. Rolling the loose ends of the flogger together like wringing a towel, I let it come down on one shoulder then the other. It was a bit more of a biting experience than a figure-eight flogging was, until you really put some strength behind your swings and let the straps bite into the subs skin.

It took a while before her skin even started to turn bright pink, showing that she was feeling it, the blood rushing to the skin. Her head lowered between hits, her shoulders flexed just before the flogger came down, and I stopped. Her reactions were telling me that it was getting harder for her to take and with what I had in mind to do next, I didn't want her pain to be too bad...yet.

Standing in front of the wall, I stared at the various canes hanging there. I didn't want it to be too intense since it was her first time with a cane, but I wanted to test her limits. I picked a flimsier one. It'd hurt, but not nearly as badly as the strong, non-flexible type.

When I returned to her, I rubbed the cane along the underside of her ass, hinting at what was coming. If she ended up liking the cane, it would excite and scare her with the impending caning. The first crack against her ass didn't get even a reaction from her except to count as I'd instructed her. Pain slut if I'd ever seen one. She took it and waited for the next one. I could tell she was crying, but she wasn't using her safe word. She wasn't begging me to stop, she wasn't even sobbing. Not until the third one did she sob, but it wasn't a body-wracking screaming cry of pain. After the fourth one, I could tell she was starting to reach subspace; her body visibly relaxed, her head lolled downward. When the fifth and final one landed and she didn't count, I knew she'd fully slipped under but not in a way that I was comfortable.

One could slip into subspace and still be responsive, most were. Sometimes if it came over the sub to quick, they'd become nonverbal or if they were in too much pain, they wouldn't be able to speak through it. While it was okay if they were in subspace, it was not if they were in that much pain, but if they overlapped and she couldn't tell me that she was in too much pain she could be gravelly injured without a way to tell me.

As soon as I'd realized what happened, I dropped the cane, unhooked her arms and carried her to the bed. Removing her arm restraint, I threw it over the side of the bed, not caring where it landed. I pulled her to my chest and rubbed her back and hair slowly, calmly, even though my insides were anything but calm.

Once she took a deep breath and realized where she was, I relaxed. As much as subs enjoyed subspace, doms enjoyed the adrenaline rush of taking control. As I answered her questions, I let my own high subside. That is, until she laughed about me forcing her to leave before she was ready to go. I didn't find it funny that she'd think I would make her leave when she was still coming down. Then again, she'd never been to subspace before or realize that it could be a very bad thing not to be nurtured right after a scene like we'd had.

She laughed uneasily and changed the subject to

her questions.

"Sure, Precious, ask your questions." I wanted to take off her blindfold. I wanted to lay her down on the bed and let her feel the weight of my body over hers, but I knew that it would only lead to temptation and make it that much harder for me not to give in to her beautiful, curvy body.

Her hand lifted to rub my chest, but instead of asking her question, she sat up and looked in my direction. "I have a question, sir."

"I already said it was okay for you to ask them," I responded, unsure of where she was going.

"I mean, I guess, I have a request then." She moved uncomfortably for a moment.

"And what is that?" I lifted an eyebrow even though she couldn't see me. I was curious.

"Since I am not allowed to wear my clothing in here, sir, I was wondering if I could ask that you not wear your shirt." She took a quick breath and continued before I could respond. "I just think it would help our connection. You get to see me, I don't get to see you. If I could feel your skin, your heat, against me, it would help me feel more comfortable."

I rose and quickly unbuttoned my shirt before pulling it off and draping it over the foot of the bed. Returning to my spot, she lowered herself so that her head was once again to my chest, a contented sigh leaving her lips at the contact.

"Thank you, Master."

Biting back a groan at the term, I hoped she couldn't feel my throbbing cock   just inches away from her. Rewrapping my arms around her, I returned to rubbing her back. "Your questions, Precious?"

"Oh, right, sir. I've been thinking about these since the last time I was with you. I was wondering how long you think I will have to wear the blindfold, sir? It's not that I mind, but I would like to see you and everything going on as well." She drew shapes on my chest with the tip of one of her fingers.

"That will depend on how well you behave. It is to encourage submissive behaviors. You experience everything more vividly when you are lacking one of your senses and sight is the easiest and most efficient to take away. Do you fear me to be impossibly ugly or some such thing? Is that why you crave to see my face?" I knew it had to be one of the reasons a woman wouldn't want to be blindfolded by a man she'd never seen.

"Yes, sir. Well, no, sir. I mean, I don't think you are ugly, but I would like to have a face to put with your voice and your touch."

"What if I let you touch my face? Then you can get an idea of what I look like, but you are not allowed to remove the blindfold. Not yet." I grabbed her hand that had been drawing on my chest and held it to my cheek before moving it over my face, when she started to move it on her own, I let go and let her explore. I didn't know that it would help comfort her much, but it was the best I could do.

"Mmm," she hummed as she rubbed her hands against my beard stubble. Then she traced the outline of my lips repeatedly.

My cock jumped, begging for her attention while I tried to hold as still as I could for her perusal. Grabbing both her hands, I had to stop her from torturing me any further. "Your second question, Precious?"

"So, I've been doing some research on this whole

BDSM lifestyle, and I'd just like to know if you have any other submissives besides me that you're training?" She sat back, her hands falling from my grasp as she kept her distance from me.

Sitting up, I reached through the dark before grazing her shoulder. My hand slid up her shoulder to grasp the back of her neck, pulling her gently forward until we were practically nose to nose. "Precious, I don't have any other submissives. Before you caught my eye, I hadn't had a submissive in a long time. I was trying to deny who I was, who I used to be, but everything about you shouted for my dominant side to take over and make you mine. As much as you are surprised by our connection, I am as well. While I am teaching you the ways, I also want you to know you are very special to me." I don't know why I told her so much, but it came out so easily I couldn't hold it back. I wanted her so damn much, but we both had our own issues and I didn't want them to get in the way of what could very well be the woman meant for me.

"Can I ask another question, sir?" she hesitantly asked, her nerves in her voice.

"You aren't satisfied with your two questions?" I loosened my grip on her neck.

"I am, sir. I just don't understand why you picked me. Why me? What was it about me? I'm nothing special. There are much prettier women, women who are already trained to be your perfect submissive, women who wouldn't be so difficult and time consuming." Again, she pulled away from me.

"Precious, that's exactly it. Don't you see? You are special because you will be trained just for me. You will be the only person who knows exactly how to please me, as I will learn exactly how to give you what you need and want. Even with a trained submissive, it takes time to build a relationship that both parties are comfortable in." I paused trying to figure out how to explain it more to her.

"But we don't have sex," she added quietly.

"That's where most people are incorrect in their assumptions about BDSM relationships. It's not about sex. It's about finding pleasure in pain or being tied up or whatever your kink may be. If both partners agree to sex, then sex may occur, but it is not necessary," I informed her.

"Oh. I see." She moved off the opposite side of the bed. "Would you like to inspect my ass now, sir?"

"Yes." I wish I'd turned off the lights, but I'd moved so fast to make sure she was okay that I didn't think of it. I knew she was growing weary of the blindfold and not being able to see. Walking around the bed, I ran my hand down the length of her back before hooking my fingers in the sides of her panties. With one swoop, I pulled them down to her ankles. She let out a soft gasp, but didn't move. Tenderly, I ran my fingers along the lines that were still evident across her ass where the cane had come down. She'd have bruises from the cane, unlike the crop. Good. I was glad she'd have something to keep me on her mind over the next couple of days. "You will have some difficulties sitting over for a few days. I want you to think of me every time you feel the pain from it. Remember how it felt to soar in subspace because of me."

"Absolutely, sir," she said with a smile on her face.

"You were a good girl today. I look forward to the next time." With that I made my way to the door on the opposite side of the room and closed it with a loud snick so she'd know that I had left the room. It was always a task to make myself leave her, but it wasn't fair to make her keep the blindfold on for too long as it could disorient her and be a bad thing. On the other hand, I enjoyed having her in my arms all the same.

I grabbed my bag that carried an extra set of clothes in it and escaped through the back entrance of the building. I didn't want her to see me walking around the front of the club. The gift I had arranged to have left for her had me excited to hear from her. I'm sure it would be a surprise, but I wanted to see her wearing something of mine. The bruises would do a good job of keeping me on her mind for the next couple of days, but they would heal and go away. The gift I left wouldn't. It was my way of claiming her even if she wasn't aware of it. One day I would explain it to her, but she was still quite new in the scene and I didn't know how she'd react to me wanting to collar her.

Chapter 11

Alix

Hearing the door close after Master J left, I stood and pulled my panties back up. After everything that had gone on, I was still a little off-balance, trying to wrap my head around it. Walking around the bed, I looked for anything else that I could take as a reminder of our time together. The ribbon my wrists had been tied with lay on the floor. Quickly grabbing it, I glanced once more around the room. A slim wooden cane was on the floor — the cane he'd used — but that would be too hard to sneak out.

Returning to the small dressing room, I found a note waiting along with a square package. Holding the package in one hand, I pulled the note from the envelope.

> *Precious,*
> *This is a gift for you to wear and remember*
> *me by. Keep it close to you just as I will keep*
> *memories of our time together.*
> *Already anticipating our next time,*
> *Master J*

The sweet tone brought a smile to my lips as I carefully pulled off the top of the box, unsure of what I was going to find. Inside was a beautiful single strand of pearls nestled in blue velvet. Slowly, I pulled the necklace out and set the box aside before draping them around my neck. Pausing to admire the gift in the mirror, I ran my fingertips over the glittering white spheres. Never in my life had I been given such a beautiful and expensive piece of jewelry, or any gift really, let alone from a man I hardly knew.

Stepping into my clothes, I couldn't help but peek at the mirror to see the gift Master had given me. Once fully dressed, I faced the mirror again. Even though it was a simple necklace, feeling their weight against my skin, seeing their shimmer in the mirror made me feel more beautiful than made sense. After running my fingers through my hair, I pulled open the door to the hallway. As I made my way toward the front, I could hear the quiet hum of voices along with the occasional scream or moan from the main room. It was easy to forget there were so many other people in the building when I was alone with Master. He made me feel like I was the only person in the world when he was around.

We hadn't known each other, but he somehow managed to put my mind and body at ease more than ever before. He was also so careful and precise with his actions, never once hurting me more than I could take, more than I was begging for deep down. How he managed to read and understand my body better than even I did, I didn't know. It didn't matter as long as he continued doing it. That was all I cared about.

Not to mention after each time we met, he let me get little pieces of information about him. I gobbled up every single niblet he gave me too. The way he held me so tenderly was exquisite as well — like he didn't want to let me go. Maybe he felt the intense attraction that I did, but he still refused to react and satisfy my other needs.

By the time I got home I was exhausted, so I stripped naked and fell into bed. The next morning, I couldn't help but keep touching the pearls and smiling as they reminded me of Master and the night before.

As I stepped into the shower, I glanced over my shoulder to see my ass in the mirror. There were five distinct lines straight across my ass that were sure to turn into beautiful bruises. They were still bright red welts that I knew were going to make sitting down most of the day interesting. There were other larger marks on my back from the flogger, but not as severe as the marks from the cane.

I took more time than usual picking out what I was going to wear to work, eventually settling on a silk dress that I'd never worn before. I hoped the silk would be cool on the hot marks and help me make it through the day.

Thankfully from the moment I arrived at work until it was nearly time to leave for the day, the phone never stopped ringing. The non-stop running around made it much easier to keep my mind off the night before and the marks still burning my flesh. Just as I started to close down my computer and get ready to leave, I remembered that it was one of the nights John came in.

Sitting back in my chair, I waited for a few minutes and wasn't disappointed when I saw Jennifer perk up at her post behind the desk. John stepped into view with his casual, lazy gait that was sexy as hell. He spoke to her for a moment and when she turned away, he tapped his fingers on the top of the desk before turning and locking eyes with me. It was like he knew I'd be there, waiting for him, watching him.

One side of his delicious mouth tilted upward,

but Jennifer returned and he turned back to face her.

For the first time all day, I felt the nagging thoughts swelling up and taking over, pushing at me. I needed to slip my hand between my legs. I had to. The longer I fought to deny it, the harder it was to breath.

As he continued to talk to Jennifer, I eased a hand up under my dress. Pushing my panties aside, I sank two fingers into my wet pussy. Angrily, I jabbed them in and out, lowering my eyes from John and Jennifer. I didn't want to be doing it, but ignoring the thoughts and craving was nearly impossible. The faster I got off, the quicker I could move on. Roughly, I pinched my clit, biting down on my bottom lip to keep from shouting out at the pain that radiated from it, but the sweet, hot, burn that followed had me thrusting my hips against my hand. The welts on my ass and back, pressed harder against the chair, adding a new and delicious sensation to my forbidden play.

Just as I had nearly reached an orgasm, I glanced up and nearly fell out of my chair when I found John standing just feet from my window that looked over the lobby. His arms were crossed over his chest and an extremely pissed-off look flowed over his handsome face.

My hand pulled from my body and I wiggled my skirt down from where it had risen in my rush to ecstasy. My face flamed red as I tried to ignore the incredibly embarrassing situation. I'd been caught, no doubt about it. It was only a matter of time, I'd known that. Hell, I'd been fired before for masturbating at work and having sex at work, but that was before. I didn't want to admit that my addiction was back to the same level it had been. It was too late; he would most likely tell management and I'd be without a job again.

Fighting back the tears and guilt, I grabbed my purse from the bottom drawer and quickly locked my door before fleeing out the employee entrance. I would have to walk all the way around the building to get to where I parked, but I didn't have to face John or anyone else he might be sharing what he'd seen with.

Opening the driver door, I plopped down in the seat only to cry out from the pain that lashed through the welts on my ass. I was so stupid. How could I not have spotted it before? Not admitted how bad I'd gotten. Driving recklessly, I sped home as tears ran down my face. Sinking against the locked door, I finally let it all out. Screaming and crying, I slapped at my thighs angrily. It was my fault. *My* fault. No one to blame but myself.

I slapped and punched my thighs until I was too tired to carry on, but the tears continued to roll down my cheeks as I sobbed. Memories from the past came rushing out of the box that I'd locked them away in.

The cold, ruthless hand wrapped around my throat, his vile stench suffocating me while the weight of his body on mine made it hard to draw in a breath at all.

Shaking, I drew my knees to my chest and dropped my head down as I cried for an entirely different reason than only moments before. My heart felt like it was going to claw its way out of my chest while my lungs burned for a good, deep breath. It'd been over three years since the last time the memories had surfaced — since they'd last held me paralyzed in their grip.

My phone beeped in my purse next to me, but I couldn't force my hand to grab it.

Time passed while I sat there; my butt had gone numb long ago. Nothing was more important than sitting there, arms wrapped around my knees, comforting — protecting— myself. Numerous times, my phone beeped, but my hands and arms refused to move to get it. As I slowly managed to push the terrifying memories back into their locked box, my heart slowed, my breathing returned to normal and I regained the use and control of my body.

Tugging my purse to my lap, I slid my legs out and leaned my head against the door as I blindly dug around for my phone. Of course, it was at the bottom under everything else in there. I had numerous messages along with a missed call, but no voicemails. Swiping across the screen, I found that all of them had been from Master J. Without reading any of the texts he'd sent me, I sent one of my own.

Can you meet tonight?

I knew it was late, but before I could put my phone down I had a return message.

Just tell me when.

I can be there in 15.

I'll be there.

Making a quick stop in the bathroom, I wiped the makeup from my face and pulled my tangled hair into a ponytail before heading to the club. There was no one waiting out front or inside the door. I left my purse on the counter. If someone wanted to steal it, let them. I didn't care. There was no one around that I saw. It had to be near midnight though so I wasn't too surprised, when I broke down it took hours for me to recover. I went to the same room I'd been left at during previous visits. Opening the door, I was surprised to find the door to the inner room open. He was waiting for me. I could feel it in the air. Indecision filled me — was I still supposed to strip or go straight in since the door was open?

"Come in and kneel. Now." Master J's voice came from the room.

Averting my eyes, I walked straight to my spot and lowered myself down to my knees.

"This is an unexpected surprise. What made you want to meet tonight?" His shiny shoes stepped into my view, standing shoulder width apart.

"Nothing, sir." I swallowed hard. I didn't want to open that part of myself to him — to anyone, ever. Some secrets are better off never shared.

"Don't lie to me, girl. You don't tell me you want to meet right away if there isn't something going on." Those shoes stepped out of my view and I strained to hear where he was going.

"I just needed the escape you gave me last time. Sub space or whatever you called it. I need it, sir." I didn't know what else to do. When his name had popped up on my phone, it was my gut reaction. Obviously I didn't think it through because he was asking questions I didn't want to answer. I should've just waited a day or two before setting up another meeting.

"What are you running from?" His palm smoothed over my head as he stepped behind me. "Don't say 'nothing' or I'll walk out *right* now."

"The past, sir." I shivered as tears filled my eyes. I didn't want to talk about it. I wanted to escape it. That was why I was with him.

"What about today made your past come up?" he asked before gently pulling the tie out of my hair.

"Sir, I don't want to talk about it. I just want to

forget." I lifted a hand to wipe away the tear that escaped even though I was fighting to keep them back. I didn't want to relive the embarrassment, the humiliation that came with the thoughts of the past. How undesirable I felt. The pain that had been pounded into me repeatedly by my rapist. The rapists that no one believed me about.

"Oh, Precious. I'll help you forget. If you tell me what I'm asking." His long fingers ran through my hair, delicately untangling it.

"I got caught masturbating at work by someone. That person will most likely tell my boss and I'll lose my job," I sputtered out trying not to focus on it. It was the easiest, least painful answer.

"So you are upset that you might lose your job? Or that someone saw you doing something you knew you shouldn't have been doing at work? Or do you not care that you were risking your job for pleasure that you should've been getting from me?" His voice lowered an octave, letting me know he wasn't happy with me.

"I hadn't been thinking at all, sir. Not about you or my job. It's an impulse thing. A compulsion." I dropped my chin to my chest in utter humiliation.

He didn't speak. I could still feel him standing behind me, his hand in my hair. The silence filling the space between us was thick and choking.

"I have a confession, sir," I blurted out before thinking it through. I wanted to air part of my dirty laundry I'd been holding onto for so long.

"Go ahead." He removed his hand from my hair and stepped back, removing his warmth.

I had to do it on my own, without his support. "I'm a sex addict, sir. I can't help it. I get this feeling that can't be ignored and I have to masturbate. Don't laugh. God, please don't laugh. It's the honest truth. I can't help it. I fight it, I struggle with it and yet, my body gives in and does it anyway. I hate that I do it, I hate that it controls me. I've been through rehab and the twelve steps, the whole she-bang. Then my eye got caught by this man at work and even though I haven't given into compulsive behaviors or masturbating in years, it's like it never left. I know I need to get help. I will get help. It's just awfully embarrassing and everyone laughs when you try to tell them about it. They think it's a joke or that I just like doing it or the feeling..."

"Stop." He cut me off as I continued to ramble with tears streaking down both cheeks. "I understand. Guess it's a good thing I didn't want to fuck you. Heaven only knows what you have or how many men you've slept with."

His voice was harsh and cut to straight to my heart. My cheeks turned red as I bit down on my bottom lip, trying to hold back the anger that built within. I was angry at myself for being such a failure. Angry with the situation I was in and that I likely was going to lose my job. Angry with the man I'd thought to be so different for turning on me so quickly when I'd shared something so private. My tremors of fear turned to anger.

"I'd bet you've slept with more men than you can count. Lost track because there are so many. Or do you just sit by yourself while you fill your pussy with fingers, dreaming it's a guy since none of them will touch you?" he spat from behind me.

My anger shot through the roof and I couldn't hold it back. I might be messed up five ways to Sunday, but I wasn't a doormat. No one talked to me like that. "Fuck you. You don't know what you're talking about.

You know nothing." I stood and reached for my blindfold. I wanted to see him as I tore into him, but his hand shackled my wrist and pulled it behind me as he yanked me back against his body.

"That's better. There's that fire I want to see. You aren't that weak, pathetic girl who came in here tonight. I don't want to see her. Addiction is addiction. I'll help you deal with it. I'm here to help you face your fears and come out the other side a stronger woman. Don't think I'm going to coddle you and let you wallow in self-pity. *Not happening*. Now back on your knees. Time to get to business." His voice vibrated the last of the fear from my body. My anger dissipated as quickly as it had flared up.

Chapter 12

John

I knew from the moment she ran from her office like the place was on fire that she was having a melt down. Text after text went unanswered and I worried that she'd been shoved too hard so I broke down and called her. When there was no answer, I drove to her house. I couldn't knock or ring the bell to see if she was there; I wasn't supposed to know where she lived. Slipping into her backyard, I peeked in her windows until I got a glimpse of her leaning against her front door. She was a wreck. It had to be more than me simply catching her in her office. When she'd finally texted me, I'd watched as she slowly pulled herself together enough to drive. The vibrant, full-of-life beauty I knew wasn't the one that was going to be showing up at the club. Leaving seconds before her, I parked behind the club and barely beat her to the room.

When she started to babble about her addiction, it gave me an idea to make her mine in more ways than she would even realize. I hadn't wanted to be an ass to her, but I wanted to shake her out of her pity-filled head. I knew a few harsh words would do it, anything to spark that anger I knew she held inside. It pushed back that weak, powerless part of her that the addiction preyed on. She'd nearly spit fire at me and my dick jumped and grew in my pants at her attack. Until she'd reached for that damn blindfold. I hated that damn thing and loved it at the same time. It would have to go soon because I wanted to look into her eyes while I fucked her senseless. There was still time for that. There were other more pressing issues than getting my cock in her tight pussy. I'd known she wasn't fucking around. I'd been watching her entirely too closely for her to be able to have a fuck buddy.

First, she needed to learn her lesson for masturbating at work. Didn't matter that she'd been looking at me while doing it. She needed to learn to control the impulses and push past them without giving in. If she wanted to play with her pretty little pussy while looking at me, then she could do it while I watched.

"Stand," I instructed her.

"Then why did you just make me kneel?" she spat at me.

Smiling, I grabbed a handful of her hair and pulled her head back, causing a moan to slip from her lips. "You will not talk back to me."

"Yes, sir." Her voice cooled to her normal, calm tone. I quickly slipped the blindfold over her eyes before I got too wrapped up and forgot to put it on.

"Now, stand and strip." I let go of her and stepped back so she could fumble through undressing alone. Once she'd undressed to her panties and bra, she lowered her hands to her sides and waited for further instructions. The strand of pearls I'd given her rested against her chest. The sight of them made something in my chest squeeze tight. "I didn't say to stop undressing."

"B… but..." She hesitated. After a moment of not getting a response from me, she sighed and slipped out of her bra and panties. "There. Happy?"

"Are you sassing me?" I asked, and landed a palm firmly against her red, welted cheek. She jumped, but didn't make any other outward response to the slap. "I asked a question."

"No...sir." She curled her lip, earning her a firm slap to the other cheek. Again, no reaction. "Do you like making me hurt, sir?"

"Yes. And you like when I do it." I pressed against her back, letting her feel the hard ridge of my erection. "I bet if I slip a finger in your pussy it's dripping wet for me."

"Why don't you find out?" she challenged.

Moving quickly, I scooped her up in my arms and carried her to the bed. I let go of her a few inches above the mattress, making her feel like I dropped her. Climbing on top of her, I pushed her arms above her head, clasping both her tiny wrists in one hand while shoving her chin up with my other. "You want to play rough? Let's play rough."

I had intended to take it easy on her since she'd already had a long, tough evening. Obviously that wasn't what she wanted or needed and that was perfectly okay with me. Using the straps that were already attached to the headboard, I restrained her wrists above her head before moving to restrain each ankle. I paused to admire her fully nude body as it was stretched out on the bed. Straddling her hips, I leaned forward and planted my lips on hers.

Her soft, pliant lips parted instantly, accepting my kiss. Unrestrained, her tongue and lips ate at my mouth.

I pulled back, both of us breathing fast and hard. How easily a soft, tender kiss had turned into a fiery exchange. Leaving a trail of kisses down the column of her neck, I made my way down her luscious body until I made it to the swells of her breasts that heaved with her rapid breaths. Her pebbled, pink nipples begged for attention and I sucked one into my mouth, giving it all that it could handle.

Alix moaned and rotated her hips under me. Pleas for more filled the air, but still I teased and tormented the little bud. Pulling a little metal clamp from my pocket, I placed it on her nipple, clamping down hard on the pleasure-filled bead. Instantly, Alix arched her hips and threw her head back. Repeating the same torment on the opposite nipple, I left it only after placing a twin clamp on it. A thin chain linked the two silver clamps.

Her breath was sawing in and out of her lungs as she tried to handle the pain that came from the clamps. I used the distraction to slip farther down her body, pushing her thighs apart so I could look down upon her beautiful, wet pussy. Dragging a finger up the slit in the center, I bit down on my bottom lip.

Her scent assaulted my senses. I wanted to rub my face all over her pussy and never bathe again. It was the most sensual and delicious smell I'd ever been gifted with.

Dropping my head, I used my tongue to mimic the same path my finger had just taken. Straight up the center of her.

Alix treated me with a gulp as she tugged at her restraints. Twisting and turning my head, I pushed her swollen lips open and buried my face in her pussy as I lapped up her delectable juices that were waiting for me. Using my fingers, I dipped two into her pussy as I flicked my tongue over her little clit. My fingers thrust slowly, deeply as I continued to tease her clit. The more I teased it, the more swollen and needy it got. Sitting back, I continued to let my fingers work her pussy as I looked down at her.

"Like that, do you?" I asked as I clutched one of her thighs in my free hand. I could already imagine holding her thighs in my palms while I pounded into her. Damn it. I craved this woman more than my next breath.

"I... I don't know how this helps, sir," she breathed as I crooked my fingers and found that special little hidden spot that made her hips jerk and her whole body clench.

"That is your G-spot. Ever come from playing with that?" I continued to nudge that spot, over and over.

"N… no." She panted as her body tensed, revealing she was getting close to her orgasm.

"You didn't answer me. Do you like this? Isn't this what you wanted? Me between your thighs?" I dug my fingers into her leg.

"God, yes. Yes... Don't stop. Oh, I'm. Going. To. Come." She screamed, pointed her toes, tensed all her muscles in preparation.

I quickly pulled my hand out of her and her body jerked as if I'd slapped her.

"No! What the fuck? Don't stop," she snarled at me, yanking against her restraints.

"You aren't ready to come. Only good girls get to come." I smiled and trailed a finger over her pussy lips. Settling between her legs, I kissed the inside of her knee before trailing kisses down her thighs. One soft kiss on the very top of her mound was all she got even though she squirmed and tried to entice me to give her more. Kissing up her other thigh, I reached up and gently tugged on the cord linking the nipple clamps together.

Alix cursed and bit her lip at the same time.

Leaning over her, I rested my forearms on either side of her head. My lips met her in a heated exchange as I rubbed my throbbing erection between her thighs. Her hips thrust against mine, meeting them as if I weren't still fully clothed. Biting down on her bottom lip, I smiled and moved to nibble on her earlobe. "You want that cock, don't you?"

"Fuck. You know I do. Why don't you fill my tight pussy up? I can tell you want to," she said, grinding against me.

"Oh, is that what you want?" I smiled against her cheek as she eagerly nodded her head.

Stepping away from the bed, I retrieved a dildo from the nearby drawers filled with toys. No need for lube; she was well-primed, as the wet mess she'd left on my slacks just from a little grinding indicated. Crawling up the bed between her legs, I rubbed the rounded tip along her pussy. A little pressure and the tip entered her followed by a low, almost painful moan from Alix. Clenching my teeth, I shoved the whole thing as deep as I could, not caring if it was deeper than she wanted. I pulled it all the way out before roughly shoving it all the way back in. I repeated the movement even as Alix cried out and writhed on the bed trying to reach the orgasm I'd already denied her once. Again when she reached the very peak, just about to tumble over, I yanked the toy out.

"Fuck you!" Alix screamed, clenching her hands and yanking hard against her restraints again. "I hate you. Let me fucking come."

"No." Slapping the hard dildo against her clit

repeatedly got me a few more curses from her before I shoved it back inside her. Leaving the dildo deep in her, I got off the bed again. "I think it's time we introduced something else into our little fun-filled adventure." I smiled, she cursed.

Once on the bed again, I removed the dildo and pressed the new, small, metallic toy into her pussy repeatedly. After making sure it was well-lubricated, I slid the toy lower until I encountered her tight asshole. Rimming her hole with the toy, her whole body shivered.

"Oh, you don't like that?" I continued to tease the tiny hole. Just as she opened her mouth to respond, I pressed the toy into her. The tapered toy slipped in before her body closed back around the smaller end, leaving a quarter-sized jewel twinkling on the outside.

"I'm gonna kill you," she whined, but there was no fire to her words. I brought my lips to hers again for another taste of the sweet, delicious taste that was simply Alix. It was a unique flavor and spice that could never be duplicated and was quite addictive from the first moment she'd surprised me with a kiss. As our lips dueled, tongues swirling and dancing, my fingers dipped low to once against slide into her heat. Keeping my thrusts slow, I teased her to slowly build her arousal back up to the peak.

Releasing her lips, I lowered my body so I could get an eyeful of her beautiful pussy again. That swollen, needy clit called out to me so I sucked it into my mouth, nipping at it none too gently.

Alix groaned and pressed closer to my face letting me know she liked just what I was doing to her. My fingers found her G-spot again and took vengeance on it. Rubbing it, nudging it, leading it exactly where I wanted it to go... straight toward climax. Alix tried to hold back her moans and cries, but the tension in her body told me all I needed. Once again I dropped her before she could make the leap off the cliff. She fell back exhausted against the bed, pursing her lips.

I tugged on the chain between her breasts and she gasped.

"God, just let me come, please. I'm begging. I'm dying. My body is going to explode. It's painful. Please, Master, I need it," she begged, and if my cock hadn't already been harder than stone it would've gotten there with that little plea.

"I'll make you a deal. If you make me come, I'll let you come." It wasn't a good deal. I knew I shouldn't have said it as soon as it left my lips, but my control was slipping the woman I'd dreamed of for so long begging me to make her come.

"Yes! Yes, fine," She immediately responded, making a deep chuckle slip from my lips.

I drew out my cock from my slacks and fisted it. The bastard was already leaking and ready for her. Sliding my hand over him a few times, I watched as she continued to writhe on the bed. Fuck, it was a sight I'd never forget. Tied up, soaking wet, plugged, clamped. So ready for me. I could so easily sink balls-deep in her. She'd love it, she was begging for it. No. No, she was begging to come. I wouldn't fuck her until she was begging for my cock and only MY cock.

Placing one knee on either side of her, I kneeled over her chest. Leaning forward, I braced my arm on the headboard while dragging my cock along the line of her lips. Her tongue darted out to lick at it as it passed. "Suck me off," I demanded.

Her mouth opened and she sucked me deep, making me groan. Her mouth was perfection. It wouldn't take me long to fill her little mouth if she kept up that kind of suction, taking my cock down her throat. And she did. Fast and hard, she moved her head up my length only to suck me back down and swallow around the sensitive tip of my cock. A few quick strokes later and I fisted my hand in her hair, holding her against me — my cock deep in her mouth — as come spurted from the tip of my dick. She quickly swallowed it down and even fucking moaned while doing it. I had to pull her hair to get her to release her tight suction on my dick, then climbed from the bed, still panting from the head rush her blow job gave me.

Shoving my semi-hard dick back in my pants I moved around the bed so I could slip between her thighs again. I snagged the dildo and as soon as I was situated, shoved it deep in her without warning. Fucking her fast and hard, just like she'd sucked my cock, I barely gave her a chance to build up before I reached up and released one then the other nipple clamp. The pain from their release mixed with the thrusting of the toy tossed her over the cliff. Her entire body stiffened, head thrown against the pillow, back arched as high as she could while restrained, a long, low moan escaping from her lips.

I threw the toy towards the corner to be dealt with later followed by the nipple clamps. Carefully, I withdrew the anal plug and it followed suit as well.

Chapter 13

Alix

After tossing aside all the toys, he slowly released my ankles, then my wrists, before sitting against the headboard and curling me in his lap. My head rested on the crook of his neck while he massaged my ankles, followed by my wrists. I felt like I was floating on a soft little cloud as he continued to massage blood back into my hands. Slowly the cloud drifted away and the anger started slip to back in.

He released my wrists when my body stiffened.

"I didn't like that. Don't do that again," I said as I tried to crawl off his lap. His hands firmly grasped my bare hip, reminding me that I was completely nude as my sore ass moved against the fabric of his slacks.

"Do what, Precious?" He threaded his fingers into my hair and pulled my head back. "Not let you get off? It's called punishment for a reason. You will not touch yourself again unless I give you permission. You will not get off unless I tell you to. The punishment next time will be much more severe, do you understand me?"

I ground my teeth even as his deep, commanding British tone sent shivers of excitement up my spine. "I will try, sir." It was hard, but I managed to not sneer when I said "sir".

"No, you will succeed or you will be punished. You have controlled your addiction before, you can do so again. I'm a text or phone call away should you be at a point where you don't think you can control it." His tongue dragged up the side of my neck, flicking my earlobe before disappearing completely.

"Yes, sir," I breathed. I may have gotten off not long before, but the tension he'd built wasn't fully released from the single, tiny orgasm he'd given me.

"Bend over the bed." He released me with a soft kiss to the forehead.

I moved to do as he asked and listened as he moved around the bed to stand behind me. I jumped when his fingers gently touched the welts on my ass.

"Beautiful. Absolutely beautiful. You'll have me on your mind for a few days still." The smile was clear in his voice as his fingers continued to trail over my ass.

For it being the first time I was nude in front of him, I was incredibly comfortable. Perhaps it was the fact that he didn't give me time to think about it, to get nervous about it. He'd taken control of me from the moment I'd walked in and that was the exact reason I'd texted him. I knew that he would have no problem helping me focus on the present instead of the past.

"Thank you for sharing your secret with me. I know it wasn't easy." His minty breath flitted over my cheek before he dropped a chaste kiss upon my lips. His weight disappeared, his scent faded and the click of a door shutting let me know that he had gone.

Standing, I removed the blindfold before gathering my clothes and putting them back on. The blindfold was left on the end of the bed and I let myself out. Just as on my way in, there wasn't anyone around. My purse was exactly where I'd left it.

Once I returned home, I collapsed into bed nude as I usually did after an encounter with Master J. My brain and body were too exhausted and relaxed to focus on any of the normal issues that kept me up.

The next morning, I dressed as usual for work even though my palms were sweaty and my entire body shook. I kept repeating to myself that it was just another day, nothing special. Nothing to fear. It was possible the man hadn't told anyone. And I needed to focus on that.

Thankfully, I made it all the way until shortly before John usually showed up without having the roof come crashing down on my world. Not wanting to see John, I packed up my belongings and headed out early. I was too embarrassed to see him again so soon.

But as I was walking out the front door of the hotel, I nearly ran right into him. His strong arms wrapped around my shoulders to stop me from falling or colliding with him. That incredibly sexy smile was only inches away from my own. I nearly melted into a puddle right then and there; instead my face flamed red and I jerked back from him. Murmuring excuses, I quickly rushed toward my car without looking back once.

Locking out the world, I hid in my house and pulled out my laptop. After a few relaxing breaths, I logged into the online counselor site. Nearly bailing when I recognized the name of the counselor who was on, I forced myself not to. It was the one I'd spoken with the last time.

Counselor21: How are you this evening?

BadKitty2: Not so good. Hence why I'm here.

Counselor21: So, running from the issues didn't help make them any better since the last time we talked?

BadKitty2: No way you remember me.

Counselor21: You are right. I take notes of every patient I talk to. Although admittedly I knew you'd be back so I kept yours near the top.

BadKitty2: Fine. You were right.

Counselor21: So, what brought you back? Did you get caught?

BadKitty2: Yes. Well, sort of.

Counselor21: Care to expand on that?

BadKitty2: No, but I will. The man that I've been fascinated with over the last six months or so... You know, the one I masturbated to… he caught me. I am afraid he is going to tell my boss and I will lose my job.

Counselor21: You say masturbated in the past tense. Getting caught has made you decide not to do it any more?

BadKitty2: Well, that's another thing I wanted to talk to you about. See, I met this man. His name is J. He is… helping me learn to control my impulses in a different way than I've ever tried before.

Counselor21: and this way is?

BadKitty2: A bit of Dominance and submission type stuff. I've never heard of something like that as a treatment for addiction.

Counselor21: Well, that's probably because it can easily become a new addiction or a shift in the addiction you are currently dealing with. Getting sex there instead of other ways.

Counselor21: It can also be a very dangerous environment if you aren't with someone who knows what they are doing. You can get injured or worse.

Counselor21: However, that being said, it can be an excellent way to learn to conquer your addiction. If it helps you learn how to channel the addictive feelings and not react, not respond to them, that's all that matters. Sometimes a unique route is the best way. Everyone is different and things don't always work the same for everyone.

BadKitty2: J knows what he's doing. He wouldn't hurt me. Hasn't even come close to it. In fact, he has vowed to not even have sex with me.

Counselor21: That is something that'll have to be for you to judge since I'm not there with you. Remember sex is healthy, it is okay to engage in. It's the impulsive need for it, doing things you don't want to do… There is a difference between them.

BadKitty2: I know, doc. Thanks for the chat.

And with that, I logged out of the program and closed my computer. It made me feel better to know that it wasn't necessarily a bad thing going to Master J. I didn't tell the counselor that I wasn't going to masturbate again. I didn't want to see what Master had up his sleeve if he found out I'd done it again. The orgasm deprivation had been horrible enough. I didn't want to go through that again, let alone something worse.

Feeling a bit better about everything, I cleaned my house while thinking about what I would wear for my next meeting with Master. When I wasn't thinking about the dreadful run-in with John and the embarrassment that had come from it, I was thinking about what it'd felt like to have Master's cock in my mouth, his hands on my body. Thinking about Master only made my body ache and the craving for release to flare up. Instead of giving in, I scrubbed harder and focused on cleaning each room thoroughly.

Once the house was clean, which didn't take all that long since I took time each week to scrub everything down, I went for a walk around the block. Anything to avoid being alone with my thoughts. Finally, I wore myself out enough that I knew I'd fall right to sleep, but I'd made it through the entire day without once giving in.

Upon waking, my body and mind felt rested and ready for the day. Feeling good, I dressed to impress with my flattering black skirt that made my legs and ass look great with a purple top that always made my boobs look awesome. A pair of four-inch black stilettos finished off the look. My hair flowed over my shoulders and the light layer of make-up made me feel like I was on top of the world. It would be a good day. It was Saturday, after all.

There was a big wedding taking place at the hotel and I'd been pulled in to help make sure everything ran smoothly. From the moment I dropped my purse in my office, I had someone needing one thing or another from me. Catering staff and decorators were tripping all over each other and grumbling. It was only ten in the morning, but it was clearly going to be a long day if it kept going the way it was.

Holding my shoulders back, head high, I was determined not to let anything ruin the good mood I'd started my day with. Before long, the biggest of the hotel's ballrooms was decorated and the caterers had their tables set up. The decorators headed outdoors where the actual ceremony was taking place, and the caterers disappeared to get the food prepped. My job was to make sure everyone knew where they were supposed to be. The other coordinator was helping with everyone outside; I handled all the inside staff, decoration and guests once they started to arrive.

"Whew, will you look at that fine piece of man meat?" the young woman who was helping me put the final touches on each table whispered.

Looking up, my eyes collided with a pair of familiar blue ones. Instantly my face burned and I dropped my eyes back to the table. "Oh yeah, that guy. He's okay." I shrugged, trying to hide my embarrassment.

"You are *crazy*. That suit hugs his body like a glove that is just *begging* to be removed. Mmm, I bet he's hung too. See that bulge? God," she mused to herself before grunting under her breath.

The sound made me laugh and shake my head. Some women were certainly a lot more assertive and forward than I was.

"I'm gonna go talk to him." She strutted off, flipping her hair over her shoulders.

So much for help. Rolling my eyes, I continued putting the party favors down in front of each plate at the table we were working on. I grabbed the stack of place cards she'd left behind and finished her job as well before pulling the small cart with all my supplies to the next table and continuing. I didn't really care what she did. I was no longer going to drool uncontrollably at the poor man. I'd give the girl a few minutes to distract John before I called her back to finish her job. It'd give me a few moments to gather myself.

The man was constantly popping up in unexpected places. It seemed the more I tried to avoid him, the more he was around. Never said a word to me, but always watching with that damn little half-smile tilting those luscious lips... no, not luscious. They were just lips.

Rolling my head on my shoulders, trying to release the tension that was collecting there, I glanced over my shoulder to find the girl and John in a conversation. His lips were moving as if he were talking to her, but his eyes were on me. Instead of looking away, having been caught, that smile tugged at his lips.

"Hey, you need to finish over here," I called out to the girl. I couldn't remember her name. John patted her shoulder before turning her toward me.

Throwing a wink in my direction, he spun and walked out of sight.

"Oh. My. God. You should hear his voice. It's *so* fucking hot." The girl sighed dreamily as she took the cards from my hand. "Too bad he shot me down. Oh well, I had to try."

"Hmm," was all I could come up with. I didn't care either way. I doubt he even knew my name, but that wink scattered my thoughts and made me second-guess everything. Maybe he hadn't seen what I'd been doing in my office. Or maybe he'd liked that I was touching myself while looking at him. I didn't know and there wasn't a chance in hell I was going to find out. I was already embarrassed enough as it was. Plus, how do you bring that up to a man you don't even know? Awkward.

After everything had finally been set up on the inside, I returned to my office and dropped into my seat for a quick break. My ass burned as it connected with the chair and made me smile as my hand reached for the pearls around my neck. That reminded me, I needed to check my phone to see if I'd heard from Master. I only had one message from him and it had been sent two hours earlier.

How you hanging in there, Precious?

The use of his nickname made me smile. No one had ever called me Precious or any other pet name at all.

Doing good, master. Just had a busy day.

I put my phone back in the drawer and stretched out my cramped back. Bending over those tables for so long had my back screaming for relief. I needed to find food at some point since it was well past lunch time, but that required me getting back out of my chair and I just didn't see that happening until it had to.

Jennifer came bouncing into my office with a plate in her hand. She set it front of me before plopping down in a chair on the other side of my desk. "I come bearing gifts."

"What's this?" I leaned forward and eyed the plate filled with grilled chicken and rice.

"Seems you have a little admirer. Our neighborhood weekly renter had the kitchen make that for you." Jennifer grinned, leaning forward with wide eyes. "What are you not telling me? How'd you get him to notice you? I've been trying forever."

"No idea. Really. I didn't ask for him to notice me." I said and pushed the plate towards her. "You can have it. I don't want anything from him." That was a lie, but I didn't need rumors to start or people to start looking for signs of something going on. Plus, nothing I wanted from the man could be served on a plate.

"No, no. Eat it. It doesn't matter that it's from him. Just eat, woman." Leaning back in her chair, her smile fell. "Why would you refuse a man like that anyway?"

"I'm not refusing *him*. I don't even know him. That's the problem. I've never even spoken to the man.

Plus, I don't have the time or energy left at the end of the day for a man and all their complications. They're all so needy." Truth. I didn't want a relationship. They required too much effort and tiptoeing around each other to be worth it. The single man I'd dated after rehab had wanted to know every detail of my life, share every intimate experience and I couldn't do it. There was a lot of pain and betrayal in my past, within my family and I wanted to avoid thinking about it. All it did was make want to go out to a club and find someone to make me feel. At that point in my life, I couldn't do that and when he pushed, I left. That's what I loved about Master. We met, did our thing, left. That's *all* there was to us.

"You don't have to date him. Just fuck him. I totally would. Have you looked at the man?" Jennifer fanned herself exaggeratedly with her hand.

"Yeah, I don't really do that either. It never works out like that." I didn't do casual sex because that was how my lonely addiction became a whole other addiction that was much scarier and could be incredibly dangerous. At least, that's how it'd been last time. That's what had made it spin out of control to the point that I couldn't handle it. I didn't care to control it, didn't care if I got hurt. That had been what made me go to rehab, because it'd gotten so bad.

No, it was best I stay by myself. I would rather be celibate than drag some man in off the street to fuck again. If Master wanted to fuck me, he could at any point. He was the only man I wanted to take that step because I knew he'd be the one to help me not lose myself again. My control was his. Each time we were together, I gave him more and more of myself. The more I gave, the better our time seemed to get. He knew what I needed and how to give it to me.

Chapter 14

John

Every time she signed into the online chat, I made sure it was automatically sent to me. I didn't want anyone else talking to her about her private thoughts. They were mine to know and a way for me to help her without her knowing. If it gave me the chance to keep her near me at the same time, then so be it. I wasn't lying to her, I was just making sure she was hearing what she needed to in order to keep her coming to the club.

I'd known about the wedding taking place in the hotel because I had been invited to it. Two of my clients were the couple, in fact, so I had every right to be there. Of course I would use the excuse to catch a few extra glimpses of Alix while she worked. Then the stupid little twat that was working with her strutted over and offered to help me get my rocks off instead of working. Only thing more annoying than a slutty woman was one who had no control. I hadn't given her any indication I was interested, but she still felt bold enough to try to rub her body along mine. Who knew how many other men she'd already done that to or how many she'd slept with? No thanks.

Thankfully, Alix called her back to finish working and I tossed a wink to Alix before heading to the office. My secretary had called out sick yet again, so there was a temp working in her place for the day. I hated having my schedule interrupted and having to teach the woman how to handle things that my normal secretary knew how to do. It was time-consuming and something I paid other people to do so I didn't have to. Thankfully the patients I had for the day were all regulars, so they would know the routine. I just hoped the secretary was back on Monday, since I had a whole slew of new clients coming in and was scheduled too tightly to be doing her job as well.

I had a feeling I was going to have to replace her since she was starting to call out more than she showed up. It was normal. My secretaries only lasted a year or two before getting burned out by the constant demands and unusual hours I insisted upon. Probably wouldn't hurt to put out feelers for a replacement.

The appointments were quick and uneventful. Nothing new came from them, but my patients left walking a bit lighter, having cleared their brains of stress, and at least got a second view on their issues. I didn't particularly care for office patients since they had more standard hang-ups — mommy and daddy issues, cheating spouses and the like. At least the patients I met with at the hotel or in their residences were more challenging and rewarding. Nothing like knowing you helped a couple find completion and orgasm while addressing an issue they had.

Back in my apartment, I quickly showered and changed into my tuxedo for the wedding. I was going dateless. It was much less complicated that way. Tugging on my shirt sleeves, I picked up my phone to text Alix before heading down to the party. After the night before, I felt the need to check on her, make sure she was still doing okay after such a roller-coaster of emotions in such a short time.

How was work, Precious?

> Still working. Won't be off for hours yet.

Smiling, I tucked my phone away. She would be downstairs when I got there. It would be dangerous, but it could be a lot of fun to play with her.

The area for the wedding was set up beautifully, but I expected it. The hotel was known for putting together amazing events. After a brief congratulations to the groom, I found a seat towards the back so I could watch everyone in the room. Plus, it'd give me the opportunity to slip away without many people noticing.

Slowly, the entire seating area filled with guests. Still no sign of Alix though. Once the procession started and the wedding party advanced down the aisle, everyone stood and turned to take in the bride. That's when I spotted Alix. She was standing off to the side, glancing over the bride's dress. Unlike most women, she didn't have that glazed-over look in her eye or the look of jealousy. Just before the bride took her first steps down the aisle, Alix leapt forward and fluffed out the bottom of her dress, then scampered back to her spot out of the way.

As soon as the bride had made her way past me and all eyes had moved toward the front of the church, I slipped out around the back — away from the ceremony. I'd talk to them later. I had more important things to take care of. Pulling my phone out of my pocket, I shot a text to Alix then slipped into a dimly-lit room off to the side. Taking off my jacket and keeping my back to the door, I waited for her. The door opened and the click of heels let me know she had arrived.

"Sir? I didn't expect you here." The quiver in her voice showed her nerves.

"Turn around. Put your hands on the door," I said, not turning around.

"B.. but..." she stuttered.

"Now. Don't make me ask again." My voice was gravelly with impatience. I knew we didn't have a lot of time and I didn't want to waste any of it.

The scuff of her shoes on the ground told me she had turned around as requested. Turning, I ran a hand up the center of her back until I gripped the back of her neck under her hair. Her ass looked incredibly delicious in the skirt she had on. Her hands were up on either side of her head, pressed against the door along with her forehead.

"Good girl." Brushing my scruff-roughened cheek against her neck sent a tremor running through her body and a soft moan from her mouth. "I'd really like to fuck you here, right up against the wall, knowing you are supposed to be out there watching the ceremony. Too bad you would be missed — plus what I have in mind for our first time together would take entirely too much time."

"Our first time? I thought you didn't want to sleep with me." She let out a soft laugh even as my hand slid around the front of her throat, tilting her head to the side.

"What makes you think I don't want to sleep with you?" I wrapped my lips around her ear and bit down roughly before pulling back. Another shiver ran through her as she pressed back against me. My free hand slid down her body, tugging up her skirt until I could slip my hand into her panties. Running my fingers through the wetness waiting for me, I waited for her to answer.

"You've told me you didn't want to sleep with

me. I thought you might be gay and just needed a sub to play with until you found a male sub to replace me with." Her words shocked me so much I froze for a moment before shoving two fingers roughly in her at the same time I applied light pressure to her carotid artery. A whimper slipped from her lips.

"You will be punished for that, Precious. I know you can't possibly be serious. My cock is constantly hard because of you. I hurt with how much I want to be balls-deep in your pussy. Don't tell you haven't noticed." I thrust my hips against her to emphasize my point. I released the pressure on her neck and pulled my fingers from within her.

"I didn't know, sir." I couldn't see her face, but her smile was clear in her voice.

"You think it's funny now. Just wait till I get my hands on you where I can do what I want without people being nearby." I rubbed my scruff up her neck, biting down hard. Hard enough to leave a mark, but not to break the skin. "I was going to let you get off, but you wanted to be naughty so now you have to wait."

"That's not fair," she groaned, grinding her ass against my crotch.

"Two can play games, Precious." I smiled before sucking hard just above my bite mark. Releasing the skin with a pop, I pressed the fingers that had been inside her against her lips. "Suck your juices off my fingers."

She sucked my fingers into her hot, wet mouth instantly. "Mmm," she gasped, undulating her hips.

Breathing her scent deep, I pushed off the door and pulled my fingers from her mouth. "Now, go back to work, naughty girl."

"Yes, sir." She dropped her head against the door with another whimper.

As she reached for the door, I slapped her ass. "Don't forget you'll get a special punishment if you touch yourself. Oh, and be sure you keep your hair over your neck or someone might ask why you have bite marks and a huge hickey."

The door swung open and I heard her laugh softly as she pulled her hair over her shoulder to conceal her neck before returning to work. I waited for a good while before slipping my coat back on and exiting the room. It'd been risky, probably a bit stupid because she could've easily turned around or waited outside the door for me to exit. She wouldn't though. It was part of the excitement, the allure — not knowing exactly who I was.

Standing outside the door into the ballroom, which was still locked to keep the guests out, I waited until the ceremony was over. Once you've seen one wedding, you've pretty much seen them all. Not like I was close with the couple. I'd seen them fuck just about every possible way you could on a bed, but that didn't make us friends. Showing up had been an excuse to see Alix plus I always went to weddings of my clients. It was a good way to find new clientele. Everyone knows someone who needs help in that area of their relationship. Some people are even bold enough to admit it is actually their *own* relationship that was lacking.

Finally, the doors were opened and guests were allowed inside. We were all given particular seats, so I found mine, then headed to the bar. I needed a glass of whiskey after that heated stolen moment. My cock was still hard, pressing against the zipper of my slacks, but thankfully my jacket kept it covered because I didn't think it'd be going down any time soon. Precious was going to be getting a good punishment for that little comment. Gay. Right. I wanted to fuck her more than I wanted to breathe, she just wasn't used to men that had control over their libido. When I fucked her, she'd remember it for the rest of her life.

I'd switch every now and then when I had my own issues arise that I needed an escape from, but it didn't happen often. I was much more dom than sub and my own submissive wouldn't see me submit to anyone. On the rare occasion I need to find subspace for a while, I went to Gabe and he helped me escape the memories of my alcoholic father who used me as his fuck toy then turned around and blamed me for enticing him when I'd been a mere child.

After sipping my first glass, I requested another one as the room-ful of guests was kept waiting for the newly weds to appear. I didn't have anywhere else to go, but my mind was filled with all the different things I had planned for Alix when we got to the club later. There was no mistake that I'd get her to the club after the wedding was over. She wouldn't get away without getting her punishment that night.

A bit of chatting with the other people at the bar and I got a few new contacts that might be in need of my services, as well as handing out a couple of my cards. Weddings always brought out the sappy feelings in everyone, but they also made everyone reassess their relationships, so they worked perfectly for me.

Finally the newly weds showed up and I was graced with a glimpse of Alix along with the other party planner. They stood toward the back of the room, directing the staff walking around offering bite-size appetizers between handling a feuding couple, who were quietly ushered out of the ballroom without drawing much notice. I didn't waste time; as soon as I could give my personal congratulations to the couple, I did so and left.

Returning to my suite, I tore off the suffocating tux and changed into a pair of jeans and a t-shirt, then immediately headed to the club. Alix would be tied up for a bit, but so would I getting things ready for her. I sent her a text telling her to let me know when she was done with work because I had plans for her. I didn't get a reply, but I knew she wouldn't disappoint me.

It was two hours later when I finally got a reply from her saying she was on the way to the club.

Good little submissive. I didn't even have to tell her what to do, but she'd known what I wanted. Settling in the room off my play room, I waited for her to arrive and sent her a message saying I was waiting. It didn't take long before I saw on the computer screen in front of me that she'd entered the changing room. Watching her undress was always a treat because she didn't know I was watching. It gave me a special little thrill knowing I got to see her at her most unprotected.

She'd worn a pair of black thigh-high panty hose along with black lacy panties and bra. That wasn't what she had on earlier so she must've had a change of panties in her car, or perhaps she'd gone home. Either way, she'd changed specially for me. Put on sexy lingerie just for me.

Licking my lips, I watched as she stepped into the main room and knelt down on her spot. I stood and entered the room and walked right to her before wrapping the blindfold around her head.

"How'd you know I was waiting for you here?" I asked out of curiosity as I tightened the knot on the blindfold.

"I knew you'd want to punish me for what I said earlier. Plus, I hoped you would bring me here to let me get release after teasing me at work." She lifted her chin as if she could see me through the blindfold, but I knew she couldn't. "I've ached for you since then. My panties were so soaked I had to change them."

"Or you could've gone without any." I smirked, dragging a finger over her cheek.

"I'd have been leaking down my thighs. I don't think I could handle that kind of embarrassment." Her face turned pink as she shook her head slightly.

"You just changed your panties? Here I was hoping you'd worn the whole set for me." I hooked a finger through a bra strap and pulled it off her shoulder before doing the same to the other.

"I hadn't planned on seeing you today, sir. Otherwise, I would've worn my garters. I know that you like those." A small smile curled her lips.

"I do, Precious. Very much so. I like this set too. You wear it very well." I rubbed my thumb over her juicy bottom lip that was begging to be kissed. Instead I stepped back. "Take off the bra."

She reached behind and unhooked the bra before slipping it off her arms and letting it fall in front of her knees. Her breasts were bare and beautiful as they jiggled slightly from being released from their prison.

I adjusted my cock and smiled. It was time to play.

Chapter 15

Alix

By the time the wedding was over, I had melted into my chair behind my desk. I knew Master was going to want me to meet him for my comment in the closet. I couldn't help it. That thought had entered my mind many times since I'd met him. He seemed attracted to me, but unwilling to do anything about it. Boy, his reaction hadn't been what I'd expected. I would've at least let him give me a nice orgasm before saying it if I'd thought he'd stop right away. Since my big mouth had shot off, I had to deal with wet panties and a needy pussy the rest of the wedding. It was miserable.

I was tempted to take a little break in my office or the bathroom and help myself out, but I knew Master would know. There was no way I was going to risk any more punishment on top of the one I was getting for calling him gay when clearly he wasn't. Thankfully I kept an extra pair of panties in my purse for just such occasions.

After changing them in the parking lot of the club, I went in to receive my punishment. He'd been waiting just as I suspected. As soon as my knees hit the cushion, he'd entered and the vibes coming off him nearly sucked the air from the room. Or maybe it was that I was so attuned to him and ready for my punishment.

Stripping off my bra, I waited for him to give me more instructions. I was left waiting for long, silent moments before finally he told me to stand. Once on my feet, his hand trailed over the pearl necklace I was still wearing. A hum of appreciation vibrated out of his chest.

"Do you know what these symbolize?" He asked. The heat from his body radiated to the front of my barely-clothed one.

"No, sir." I shook my head.

"Then why do you wear them?" His finger hooked in them and tugged like he was going to yank on the strand —to break it.

"Because you gave them to me, sir. They remind me of you when I have them on," I quickly answered. My hand itched to grab the necklace away from him so he couldn't take them from me.

"Good answer. It is also a sign of ownership. Consider it your training collar. Do you understand?" He dropped the pearls, but let his fingers trail up the opposite side.

"I wear this when you are training me?" I replied and shrugged. I didn't understand.

"No. When you wear this it is because you are mine. No one else is to touch you unless I give them permission. It is a training collar because I am training you in the ways of BDSM. I have a more formal collar that I want you to wear for tonight since I have something special planned, but when outside of the club this is your collar. Do you understand?" His foot steps retreated then returned. Something cold and slick touched my neck before he tugged all of my hair over one shoulder.

A solid, heavy weight wrapped around my neck as he fiddled with the backside. I lifted a hand to touch it. Leather and metal.

He stepped back and I dropped my hand. His hand glided down the column of my neck gently before wrapping around the side. Stepping close to me, he dropped kisses along my neck. "I love seeing my bite and kiss marks on you."

"I like having them there, sir." I bit my bottom lip as a rush of warmth hit my pussy. It was quite possibly the sexiest thing I'd ever experienced when he bit me. When I'd caught a glimpse of the marks in the mirror, I couldn't keep the smile off my face. Having him kiss and caress them was only that much more erotic and sexy. If this is how he was going to treat them, I wanted to have them on me all the time.

Master stepped away from me and I felt an odd tugging sensation from around my neck.

"That, my pet, is a true collar and leash around your neck. This is what you will wear whenever we are around other members of the club." His hand stroked along my hair, then cheek, as he spoke.

All I could think was that he'd said *around other members*, which meant that we were going to be leaving the room together. Instinctively, my arms wrapped around my breasts, concealing them.

"No, Precious. You will not cover up. Show off that beautiful body that is all mine. Every man in the room will want you and every woman will wish they were you." His gentle fingers pried my hands off my arms, making them drop to my side.

I didn't say it, but I couldn't stop the thought that other women would only want to be me because I was his. I knew my punishment was coming and didn't want to add to it by upsetting him.

"Stand. Follow where the leash leads you."

Following his instructions, I felt incredibly

awkward and unsteady trying to walk without knowing where I was going. After tripping twice, the pressure on the leash disappeared, so I stopped, only to feel the heat of his body radiating against mine.

"If you stop trying to figure out where to place your next step and simply trust in where I'm leading you, you will stop tripping. Trust me to keep you safe." His hushed voice vibrated over me and I nodded once before his heat disappeared and the tugging started again.

Closing my eyes, I tried to do as he asked. Trusted that my feet would land upon solid ground with nothing in my way that would trip or harm me. Surprisingly, after a few steps, it got easier. I knew he had to be leading me down the hall that I normally entered through, or one like it, since the noise of my heels on the hard floor was quieted by thick, sound proof walls.

When we exited the hall, entering a big, open room, I could feel the difference. The temperature dropped a few degrees and the hum of voices got significantly louder.

My arms itched to cover my bare breasts, but I kept them down. I wished I had pants on to wipe off the sweat accumulating on my palms; instead I only had slightly damp thighs. Even as my mind spun in a million directions and I tried to absorb where I was and what was going on, I followed Master as he led me through the room.

"Sit on your knees," Master told me, and I dropped to my knees where I stood. I could hear him talking in hushed tones with someone before I heard the creaking of leather. "Scoot forward and move to my side."

Tentatively I reached out and found his knee with a hand. I moved based on where his knee was to sit next to him. My knees hurt and my thighs were uncomfortable. I wasn't used to kneeling so long and after spending so much time in the private room before once again being on my knees sent shooting pain through my lower extremities. It wasn't so much pain that I couldn't continue sitting as I was, but if I was going to be in the same position for too long I knew I'd have a hard time walking right away.

"Precious, we are going to sit here and let everyone get a good look at my beautiful sub. Spread those gorgeous thighs. Let them get a glimpse of that sweet pussy." His voice had the thickest British accent I'd heard yet. The deep, stern tone had me biting back a moan as fire spread through my body.

Spreading my thighs, I straightened my back. I was determined not to let my nerves show. I'd never been so uncomfortable in my life, but I'd also never felt so safe. I knew Master wouldn't let anything happen to me. It was not being able to see who was there, who was looking, who was talking that made it so hard.

I lost track of time as I sat there listening to quiet voices carrying on conversations about a wide variety of topics, not just sex. In the background, there were occasional yelps and shouts that very well could have been pleasure or pain, but without having an image to go with them I couldn't say for sure. Master was talking to another male, but I'd grown bored with the topic before tuning into other conversations taking place. I made sure to keep my thighs spread and back straight even through the pain was slowly getting worse. Occasionally Master would stroke my hair or arm, but not once did he address me. A few people even stopped to comment on me sitting there, but he managed to usher them on quickly before returning to the man he was conversing with.

"Can you stand?" A hand wrapping around the back of my neck let me know he was talking to me.

"Yes, sir." I moved to stand, but found that as I had feared my legs and knees were very slow to cooperate and the pain grew worse as I finally got to my feet.

"Take a moment," Master told me, holding my elbow for balance.

It took a few moments for my legs to get circulation back and the pain to lessen. Once it did, I said, "Ready, sir."

After being led for a few steps, I was instructed to take a step up and figured I was probably on one of the many stages I'd seen in the main room before. A hot, firm hand on my lower back showed me where to go until I felt something cold and wooden pressing into my upper thighs.

"Bend over, arms above your head," Master told me.

Bending at the waist, I felt my chest come in contact with a flat surface before raising my arms above my head. A thick strap wrapped around my wrists, binding them together. Footfalls told me Master was moving around — his hand trailed over my back as he moved. That hand followed the length of a leg until it closed around my ankle. Another strap bound my ankle to the device I was draped over before he repeated the treatment on my other leg.

As soon as the final strap was secured,

effectively holding me in place, the air became thicker — harder to pull into my lungs. My mind raced to comprehend the situation and sensations. I was in the middle of a room filled with any number of people without any way to escape while being unable to see. I had to completely trust Master or else I was going to hyperventilate or have a panic attack. Not wanting to have either happen, I repeated over and over that Master would take care of me.

A cold, unfamiliar brush along the center of my back made me gasp and fist my hands. Once the trail ended at the top of my ass, it lifted from my skin. The slight displacement of air against my ass gave me a millisecond's warning before the burning slap lit up my left cheek. The impact felt familiar, almost like the crop Master had used before.

"Since you wanted to play games with me, it is time for you to find out why that is not a good idea. This will be your first punishment, so I'm going to go easy. Next time I won't be." Masters voice was rough and harsh. He was not happy. "Count them. If you miss one, I'll start over. Understand?"

"Yes, sir." My voice wavered, betraying my nerves. The warm press of his hand upon my lower back was the only comfort I got before the sharp impact fell upon my right ass cheek, leaving behind a burning sensation. "One, sir." I didn't hesitate in responding. That had long ago been ingrained in me.

Each strike was harder than the one before, but I managed to count out all ten without breaking down or finding that blissful, floating peace that helped turn pain to pleasure.

"Precious, your ass is glowing red on either side of your thong. While incredibly sexy, that was only the warm-up. Now the actual punishment starts." Master's hand gently caressed the flame burning on each cheek before his touch disappeared completely. Suddenly, his hand landed on one cheek then the other. The loud slap of skin on skin echoed in my ears as the burn shot through my entire body. Oddly, the burn from his hand was much greater than the one the crop had left.

"Sir?" I managed to whisper after swallowing back a whimper.

"Yes?" He responded right away.

"Am I counting these as well, sir?" The question allowed the burning in my ass to lessen. My mind was fighting over what I was feeling. It was painful, but not, at the same time. The shock of new sensations was the primary feeling I recognized.

"No." His terse answer was followed by a rapid succession of blows on alternating cheeks until I felt the weightlessness starting to slip over me.

I'd never been more thankful that I didn't have to keep count because I'd already lost track, and the floating sensation made everything seem so light and fuzzy I doubted I could speak as quickly as the blows were raining down. Eventually, they stopped and my ankles were released, then my wrists followed. Instead of being moved, I was simply turned onto my back before my wrists were again bound over my head.

"Mmm, yes. Floating now, aren't you, Precious?" Master's smile was clear in his tone even as I felt his hand slide down between my spread thighs, barely brushing against the center of my body. One at a time my feet were lifted so they rested on what oddly felt like stirrups. The position opened me up as Master stepped between my spread legs.

Feeling slightly disconnected from everything, it was hard for me to focus on Master. Even when his fingers caressed the sensitive skin along the crease between my legs and hips, all I could manage was a moan of agreement. The rough tug on one side of my panties made my hips jerk against Master's. His hard erection pressed against my thigh through his pants before he pushed aside my panties and stepped back. My entire lower region was revealed to Master.

"Fuck, yes. All soaking wet. So much for punishment. You loved getting your ass spanked. Let's see how much your greedy pussy can take." Pressure against my opening had me arching my back as his fingers entered my body. Feeling the stretching of sensitive tissue as he thrust them roughly in and out of my body made me groan. "Three fingers and that greedy pussy just sucks them in. How about four?" Without waiting for my response, another finger joined and the pressure increased.

Shuddering, I closed my eyes behind the blindfold. It didn't hurt, it felt good.

Thankfully, he slid them slowly in and out of my needy body.

I'd never felt so full, so wide open. My hips writhed as I met him thrust for thrust. Moans tore from my throat. My body wasn't my own, it was his to do with as he wanted. I was just there to experience the pleasure he gave. The thrusts stayed slow, but hard. Each one moved my ass against the table below me, rubbing the tender tissue. It only added another level to the intense level of erotic pleasure throbbing through my entire body. My release built but managed to stay just out of reach.

"Damn." Hot breath brushed against my neck as

Master's weight pressed down on me. His cock again pressed against my thigh as he dropped an open-mouthed kiss just below my ear. The fingers in my pussy continued their torment. Master whispered roughly against my ear, "I want to fuck you right here, right now. Feel how hard my dick is for your tight little pussy? Just seeing you take my entire fist in your dripping cunt makes me want to come. Our first time won't be in front of a crowd, though. You aren't ready for all of me yet anyway. Don't worry, though, I'll take care of your needy pussy."

Crowd? Fisting? I didn't know which scared me more. I could feel him add his thumb into the mix; instead of pain as I expected, ecstasy vibrated out from my pussy. I could feel his finger tripping against my G-spot on the front wall of my pussy even as my body struggled to embrace everything he was making me feel.

His weight and heat left me only to resurface between my thighs as his wet tongue flicked against my swollen, throbbing clit.

My thighs trembled from the stress of being so wide open for so long, but I fought to keep them open. To embrace how incredibly good it felt to have Master giving me so much pleasure. It was unlike anything I'd ever experienced, just like everything he introduced me to. My back arched, pressing harder against his hand and mouth. An orgasm unlike any I'd ever felt before was building, growing, encompassing my entire body. Just as the pleasure was about to crash over me, he moved away leaving me empty and weeping. Literally. Tears sprang to my eyes even as I struggled to hold them back. I was beyond pride, beyond caring. I begged, "Please. Please, don't stop. I'll do anything."

Without a response, Master stood between my legs, hands pressing my thighs further open as he ground his hard, cloth-covered erection against my throbbing, begging mound. His mouth latched onto my breast, sucking hard on the tender tissue just to the side of my nipple for a moment before his teeth sank deep.

A moan escaped my throat as I rotated my hips, against his still reaching for my release. My fists wrapped tight around the rope that bound them as air rushed in and out of my lungs. The denial of my epic release almost hurt. As I struggled to hold back my tears, I barely felt it as Master sank his teeth into my other breast briefly before lapping his tongue over both bites he'd given me.

I was coming to realize that orgasm denial was Master's favorite method of punishment.

Chapter 16

John

Damn. I was quickly becoming addicted to the sweet moans and sighs coming from Alix. Bringing her right to the crest of release only to back off and hear her frustration made me smile. She was learning the hard way who was in control. I was and it was easy to see that denying her orgasms was the easiest way to show her that. I was always in control. She might push me to my limits, but I wouldn't let her break down the carefully constructed walls I'd put up. I was the Master, she was the submissive. While I might give everything I had for this little woman and her wanton cries, I would be the one in charge. I had to be with her.

"Please. Please, more, Master." Even her voice was needy as she begged, rubbing her wet pussy against my erection.

"No," I whispered in her ear before dragging my tongue up the outer edge. "You will come when I tell you to come and not before. Unless you need to come so badly you won't mind taking another punishment for it." God, did I have a punishment in mind for her. It was one I'd only used a handful of times, if that. It was brutal, it was sexy and it was painful, but it taught a lesson in a way she'd never forget. I hadn't stopped thinking about her breathlessly confessing her addiction to me. While my addiction was one I was much more adept at hiding, I felt her pain. The need to do something that you didn't want to do, yet wholeheartedly wanted to do. Only another addict would be able to relate and understand what it felt like.

Grasping onto her inner thighs, I dug my nails into her flesh. She moaned and rolled her hips against me. It was clear that she was a pain slut. The crop didn't break her, no matter how much muscle I put behind it. Even using my palm took a lot to finally get her into subspace. My own palm still burned from the effort I'd put behind her spanking. She was a masochist who perfectly matched my sadist. Her body begged for me to do my worst so that it could enjoy every second of the pain I gave it. She might not understand it, but I did. I was going to make damn sure she understood why we were the perfect pair. Her body called to mine on a level that words would never be able to express. Her response to me revealed just how perfectly we were matched.

It wasn't that I wanted to *hurt* her. I wanted to cause her pain. I wanted to control her. I found pleasure in the way her body enjoyed everything I did to it. She didn't scream out and crawl away from me like I was a freak. She bowed her back and pressed her hot pussy against me while begging for more. She needed what I could provide her with, she wanted what I yearned to do to her. I needed what she blessed me with, the control. That was what made it different than hurting her. It was something I desired to give her and something she wanted. If I had my way, and I'd do my damnedest to do it, she would never regret what we had and did. That was the difference.

My cock was beyond throbbing, begging. It straight up hurt with the need for release. Glancing around at the crowd we'd gathered, I knew that I couldn't give in just yet. While I had no problem with on lookers, there are somethings that are meant to be kept secret and special between a couple. The first time I got my dick in her would be just for us. I wanted it to be something both of us could recall with vivid details, an experience without any interruptions or outside noises taking away from it.

Reaching up, I released her wrists from their bonds before scooping her off the table. Instantly, her arms wrapped around my neck as her face dipped into it. I carried her off the stage without a word to anyone. The only person that mattered at that moment was in my arms. I needed to give her some much-deserved aftercare. Alone.

Once in my private room, I set her delicately down on the bed, her head on a pillow. Turning off the lights, I felt my way to the bed. Even with my painfully hard cock begging me to give in, I refused to have sex with her until I could see her beautiful eyes while filling her for the first time. Upon returning to the bed, I gently slipped the blindfold off before lying on the bed next to her nearly nude body. Pulling her close to me, her soft sigh of contentment let me know she'd more than enjoyed everything I'd done to her. After a short period of holding her to me, her delicate hands soothed up my chest, pushing up my shirt as they went.

Her lips pressed against my chest in a kiss at the same time she pressed her hips against mine. Reaching down, I tugged on the thin material still wrapped around one of her hips. I'd been so desperate to get at her pussy earlier I didn't waste time tearing away both sides, but it was a completely different atmosphere with just the two of us. Dropping the tiny scrap of fabric off my side of the bed, I knew I would retrieve it after she left to add to my collection of her clothing left from our time together.

"Master…" Alix's soft voice filled the darkness.

Leaning up on an elbow, I looked down at her through the veil of shadows cast over her face. They were thick enough that I couldn't make out any distinct features, but I had looked at her enough to know exactly what she looked like.

"Please don't leave me like this. I need you. I need to feel you." Her palm grazed over my chest until she could pull my shirt over my head.

Even knowing it wasn't a good idea, I helped her get it off. As soon as I settled back onto my elbow next to her, her hand wrapped around the back of my neck, pulling me down with a surprising amount of strength to meet her lips in a heated kiss. Pulling back, I bit hard on her bottom lip. The coppery taste of blood met my taste buds. Running my tongue over her lip briefly, I savored her moan before leaning back on my elbow. "Naughty sub," I growled before reaching for her necklace.

Her hand grabbed mine before I could take it off. "What are you doing? I'm sorry. I didn't mean…"

"Just wait and see," I told her as I removed the pearl necklace and set it aside. Licking down her neck, I nipped playfully at her breasts and luscious pink nipples. Her moans had me moving farther down her body until I came to her pretty, damp pussy. A soft drag of my tongue up her slit showed me just how needy my Precious was. Using my fingers, I spread her lips to get better access to the swollen bud filled with nerves. With just the tip of my tongue, I traced design after design around the bud never touching it. The more I played, the louder she moaned and groaned. Her hips arched off the bed as she tried to direct me to where she needed me.

Continuing to torture her, I used one finger to

slowly trace her slit and rim her opening. A smile slipped over my lips when both her hands grasped the back of my head, her nails digging in as she continued to try to force me to go where she wanted. Finally, I sucked her hard, tender bud into my mouth, flicking it repeatedly with my tongue. Just as she was about to come, I released it. Before she could fully calm, I dipped two fingers into her pussy. Curving them upward, I found the pea-sized pleasure center that hid there. As soon as my fingers pressed against it, her entire lower body lifted from the bed. Her thighs closed on my head, nearly suffocating me.

She was trying to ride my face, but I pulled my mouth off her and shook my head at her even as my fingers continued to tease her.

Again as she was about to come, I pulled my fingers from her. Her curses made a deep laugh slip out before I could stop it. She didn't mean any of them, I knew she didn't. It was the painful need to come that was controlling her. One that she needed to get used to ignoring and learn to live with.

Picking up the necklace, I threaded it around her clit. My thumb rested just below it with the strand of pearls running along either side of her beautiful, swollen clit. "Now, Precious, you will see why I gave you pearls, and why I am the only one that gets to touch them." I had many things that I wanted to do with the necklace, but first she had to learn that they were more than just a necklace or collar. Holding both sides of the strand in my other hand, I pulled one side. As the necklace slid around my thumb, the pearls bumped into her clit over and over as each slid by. Pulling on the other side had the same effect, but the necklace moved the other direction around her clit and my thumb. It only took a few tugs on the necklace before she was bucking against me, which made me stop. "You have to hold very still," I instructed her. As soon as she was quiet again, I moved the necklace from one side to the other.

Her nails dug into the mattress. Her moans were nearly painful to listen to. Gasping for breath, she said, "Please, let me come, Master."

Sliding the necklace back and forth a few more times, I knew she was on the edge and wouldn't be able to hold off much longer. "Come, Precious."

As the words left my lips, her entire body tensed as one long, loud scream filled the room. Her fists tugged up on the sheets as every muscle in her body contracted while her orgasm washed over her.

Removing the pearls, I set them to the side again and moved to lie next to her. My cock didn't like that I pulled her to my chest to hold her close, not seeking release of my own. I would relieve myself when I was alone. It wasn't my favorite thing to do, but I needed it after such an intense play time with my beautiful Precious.

Running my hand up and down her back as I held her, I felt her breathing slowly return to normal.

"Master…" Alix's hesitant voice was accompanied by a burst of hot breath against my chest.

"Yes." I smoothed a hand over her locks even as one arm continued to firmly hold her.

"May I pleasure you?"

I hadn't expected her to ask such a thing. The fact that she asked instead of doing as she wanted told me she was learning more about being a submissive. As much as I wanted to have her sexy mouth wrapped around my cock, I wasn't ready to give up that part of my control just yet.

"Not tonight, Precious," I murmured. She let out a groan in response.

"Please! You have pleasured me. I haven't come so hard in my life. Let me at least try to give you a fraction of that kind of pleasure," she begged.

My cock eagerly jumped in my jeans, accepting her plea. Holding her entirely nude body against mine wasn't helping the blood leave that part of my body, but I refused to release her from my grasp until I absolutely had to.

"No." I shook my head to emphasize my point.

After a moment of quiet, her hand slowly slipped down my chest until it bumped against the top of my pants. Maybe I was wrong about her learning how to be a submissive. When her fingers fumbled with the button on my jeans, I dug my fingers into her back.

"What are you doing, Precious?" I asked even though it was apparent she wasn't waiting for me to allow her to touch me in such a way.

"Exploring, sir." She shrugged her shoulders even as her fingers successfully unbuttoned and unzipped my pants.

"The answer was no," I repeated, but still did nothing to stop her. I knew I should stop her. She wasn't following my directions, but the pain in my balls was bad enough I would let her "explore" a bit so I could use the touch of her hands on me when I took care of matters on my own.

"I know." Her hand dipped under my boxer briefs until she found the hot, hard cock waiting for her.

"If you continue, you will be punished." It nearly hurt to say the words, but she would learn to submit even if my body didn't agree with it. Biting my lip, I barely held back a groan when her hand circled around the throbbing head of my cock.

"As you wish, sir." The smile in her voice was evident. She knew exactly what she was doing and didn't mind getting punished to get her way.

"So be it." I exhaled. My body was at odds. Wanting to let her give me what she apparently needed to at any cost — I certainly wouldn't mind getting some relief in the process. Then on the other hand, I knew I should stop her, not let her get her way. Keep my control of the situation, control of my body.

"Sir? Can I ask a favor since I will already be getting a punishment?" she breathed against my chest.

"I agree to hear the request." I didn't want her to mistake my words.

"Will you show me how you like to be touched? I want to make sure you like what I'm doing." Her head ducked and I'd guess she was dropping her eyes in embarrassment.

"I don't think you could make it not feel good. I'll tell you if something doesn't work." I inhaled sharply when she suddenly tightened her grip around my cock and tugged along the length before sliding down to the base.

"Good?" she asked with a smile in her voice.

"Yeah…" I groaned as she did it again.

When her hand suddenly released me and she climbed off the bed, I pushed up onto my elbows to try to see what she was doing. Her hands grabbed the sides of my briefs and jeans to pull them down —with a little help from me. As soon as my cock and balls were sprung from their confinement, she released my pants. Moving to kneel on either side of my calves, her palms smoothed up my thighs. As soon as her fingers grazed the small patch of hair I kept neatly trimmed between my thighs, her nails gently dragged over my tight ball sack. I could almost come just from the feeling of her finally touching me where I'd wanted her for so long.

"How is that, sir?" She asked, repeating the movement.

Chapter 17

Alix

I'd never been so dominated, so controlled in my whole life. I'd also never come as hard as I did when he was the one who told me when I was allowed to come. No matter what happened between Master and me, I would never be the same. I couldn't be. I'd learned too much about myself. I might not have known him for long, or been introduced into the whole scene in a traditional way, but I couldn't go back to how I'd been before. Every fiber of my being demanded that I do as Master said; even if I pushed his rules from time to time, being under his control was heavenly. Sometimes it felt too one-sided. I wanted to make him feel as good as I did. I needed to make him want me on the same level that I needed him.

I had felt his erection numerous times when we'd been together, but he had never tried to sate that need, not with me at least. After the scene with him, after the pearl experience, I literally couldn't leave until I knew that he got off from me. It was devastating to think that he might be going to another to help him with it when I was more than willing. If he continued to deny me, pushing me away, I knew it would be time to break out from under Master. As much as I learned and discovered from him, my peace of mind needed more. I was willing to go without knowing what he looked like or what his name was, but my patience with that was wearing thin. If things were to continue as they were, I needed to have more say, more input in the situation.

The more I thought about his secrecy, the more it bothered me. Why was it so important? He had so much he could hold over my head that I wouldn't expose him to anyone, but still he held his secrets. It was frustrating and worrisome.

Deciding I'd try to win at least one of the battles in my head, I seized the opportunity to try to please him. I'd never so much as felt his bare cock before and that was going to change.

Kneeling over the shadowed form of Master, I ran my nails over his balls again. While I knew he had to enjoy doling out pain, he didn't seem to mind a little bit of it himself; still, I kept my nails light. Once he confirmed that he did indeed enjoy what I was doing, I bent at the waist, bringing my face close to the throbbing, hot cock standing at attention. Holding a hip in each hand, I flicked my tongue out over the tip of the swollen flesh. Master sucked in his breath giving me chills. I was in charge when in that position. I was surprised he let things go as far as they had, but I wasn't going to give him time to reconsider.

Not waiting another moment, I sucked his erection as deep into my throat as I could — hitting and pushing past the back of my throat so I could swallow every inch of him. Having no gag reflex was a beautiful thing, too bad the person that taught me had been an unwanted lover. Master agreed from the groan that filled the air. Both his large hands grasped my head, fingertips digging in since he couldn't hold my hair. Slowly, I moved back up the long, thick shaft. Using one hand, I held onto the base of his shaft, making sure he stayed right where I wanted him before once again taking him all the way in.

"Fuck, that feels good. No one has ever taken me so deeply in their mouth," Master muttered almost to himself. His hips jumped as I swallowed around him, squeezing him tighter. "Don't stop." He said when I released him from my mouth completely.

"Mmm. Do you like my mouth, Master?" I purred, dragging my tongue along the bulging veins in his shaft as my hand used the left-behind saliva to slide up and down. Slowly. I wasn't rushing anything. I wanted him to last. I wanted to make it better than anyone had ever been for him before. Who knew if I'd ever get the chance to do it again since he'd barely let me touch him any other time.

Master pushed up on his elbows again and reached behind my head to yank the tie from my hair. The strands fell around my shoulders before he sank one hand into it, pulling my face to his. His soft lips pressed against mine for only a moment before his tongue speared into my mouth. There was no asking for permission; once again, he took what he wanted and I was more than happy to give.

His tongue dragged against the inside of my upper lip, tasting me in the most unique kiss I'd ever received. Yanking back on my hair, he kissed along my jaw until he reached my ear. His voice was deep and very distinctly British as he breathed against my ear. "You taste better than anything else I've ever had in my mouth. And I absolutely fucking love the way you suck on my cock." Slamming his mouth to mine again, his teeth hit mine, but I didn't mind as his tongue was once again invading my mouth.

All the while, I let one hand keep the slow, teasing rhythm on his erection. As much as I savored his kisses, I wasn't done with the prime piece of flesh I'd been granted either. It was my turn to break the kiss. Even though his fingers twisted my hair tighter, making me moan and heat flared between my legs, I pulled my lips from his. "I'm not done, sir." Dropping my head to his lap, his hand still tangled in my hair, I took him back into my mouth, moving my hand to cup his balls as I picked up a rougher, faster suction on his cock. If he let me, I was going to make him come. There was nothing more I wanted at that very moment. I'd bargain for it if he tried to keep me from going that far.

The longer he let me keep him in my mouth, dragging my lips upon his heated flesh, the more confident I became. When his hips started to thrust to meet my lips, I dropped my hand on his balls to press two fingers into the sensitive skin right behind his sack. Never stopping the up and down movement of my head, I added a little pressure and rotation to that sweet spot.

"Shit. Shit. Shit," Master rasped. His hand was tighter than ever in my hair, pulling it from the roots, but I refused to stop because of a little pain. When his other hand lifted from the mattress to cup my jaw, thumb brushing over my cheek as I moved, my eyes rolled back in my head. It was such a caring touch when I'd least expected one. "Precious, I'm going to come." The hand in my hair pulled harder, telling me to release him.

Acting as if he hadn't just tried to move me, I continued what I was doing, more determined than ever. The pulsing on the base of his shaft warned me right before I got a throatful of his wonderful release.

His deep moans, the thrusting of his hips and that damn hand still gently holding my cheek nearly made me come too. I waited until he released my hair to let him slide out of my mouth.

His wet, already-softening dick slapped against his stomach. "Fuuuuuuuuuck." The single, drawn-out word was all I needed to know that he more than enjoyed what I'd done.

"Thank you, Master," I murmured before slipping off the bed and out of the room. I knew I should've waited until he recovered and took over again, but I didn't. I turned just as I opened the door to the dressing room and tried to get a glimpse of Master's face, but he'd already turned on his side so all I got was an eyeful of his nude body. He had dark brown hair. That was a new fact that I learned at least, not that it was all that special. Many people had hair that color and similar hair styles, but it was something.

Master stirred, probably from the light still spilling into the room, so I quickly shut the door. Inside the small dressing room, I quickly replaced my clothing, or what I still had from it. I was going to have to go panty shopping if he was going to keep destroying the ones I had. It made me smile to remember what had happened in the crowded room. While I should probably be embarrassed or nervous about who saw me, I couldn't stir up those emotions, not standing just on the other side of the door from the man who'd seemed so hungry to get at me there was no time to simply remove the tiny garment.

Once I had dressed, I noticed I was missing my necklace. I'd been so occupied with getting a glimpse of Master and finally getting to make him come, I didn't even think to try to find them in the mess the bedding had become. Tapping my foot, I debated going back to get them or leaving without them. It was a hard decision, it really was. Did I leave the one thing Master had given me that not only served as my link to him, but also was a symbol of his ownership of me? Or did I return to the room when I hadn't been instructed to? Then again, I left the room without him telling me to, so it couldn't be such a bad thing, right?

Sighing, I put my forehead on the door. Finally, I gave in and opened it. To my surprise, the bed was empty. Completely. Not only was the delicious naked man that had been there only moments before gone, but so was all the bedding. The room was brightly lit and there was no sign that I'd spent an unknown amount of time in there with Master. I had to blink numerous times to let my eyes fully comprehend. Stumbling backwards, I slammed the door only to open it again. Still looked the same.

Frowning, I brushed my hair behind my shoulders. They caught upon cold metal though. Jumping in front of the mirror hanging on the wall, I saw that I hadn't been left without a symbol of ownership or without something to remember Master by. I still had the leather collar wrapped around my neck with the metal chain hanging from it that he must have used as the leash. Running the tips of my fingers over the soft leather, I remembered what it'd felt like for him to put it on in the first place. A contented sigh left my lips as a smile brightened my face. Yes, it would be okay if I left without my pearls. I might prefer them since they caught less attention, but I could work with the leather collar for a few days until I managed to meet with Master again. Maybe he'd give the pearls back to me. Or even better, let me experience his special kink again. Never before had I known pearls could be used in such a naughty way, but I would never forget, that's for sure.

Making my way back to the front, I picked up my purse before returning to my car. As I walked toward it, I heard footsteps behind me, but they didn't sound close or menacing since there were other people in the area. Once I reached my car, I turned to look over my shoulder to see if I could find the owner of the trailing footsteps, but there didn't appear to be anyone close by. Rubbing at the bumps that popped up on my arms, I closed myself in my car, making sure to lock the doors before I put the key in the ignition. As I pulled out of the parking lot, I kept my eyes open as I searched for someone that could be hiding or lurking, but there was no one. It had to just be me being on edge because of the night's experience. It always took me a while to feel "normal" again after time with Master.

Once I got home, I stripped and fell into bed completely naked since I still hadn't replaced the torn panties, which only brought back to mind everything I'd experienced in one short night. Master had given me a collar, which, although slightly odd, made me feel calmer in a way. It's hard to explain what a small piece of leather did for my inner crazy — almost like it was our strange way of saying we were boyfriend and girlfriend or exclusive, although we'd always been.

Groaning, I rolled onto my side, rubbing the cool sheets next to me. The collar was still around my neck along with the chain. I knew I should remove the chain so I didn't end up in a tangled mess as I slept, but I didn't want to remove anything that Master had given me.

On top of the collar, I'd had my first experience with fisting, doing naughty things in front of a crowd that not only knew what was going on, but was blatantly watching. Then to add the cherry on top of the night I got to take Master's beautiful cock into my mouth, my hand, my soul. Okay, maybe that was a bit far, but it was an experience I wouldn't be forgetting any time soon. All that control. All that strength and determination. I had broken through it. Me. Plain, boring, strange me. As much as I enjoyed it and he had seemed to as well, I knew that he wouldn't be letting it happen again anytime soon since he'd fought so hard not to give in.

My body craved getting him inside me. Feeling all that muscle and man on top of me, thrusting that large, hard cock into me. Everything about him was addictive, even the smell of his arousal leaking out of the tip of his cock. The musky scent of his sweat was more like a cologne made exclusively for me. It showed me just how hard he was working and how much he wanted me in return even if the words didn't leave his mouth.

Laying nude in bed with thoughts of Master's hard cock plunging into me normally would've had my hand between my legs, sating that need that was pulsing between my thighs. Oddly though, I felt none of that desire. Mainly because I knew that I'd have to answer for breaking the rules. As often as I purposefully broke or pushed the limits, I was determined not to allow myself to fold on this one. I feared that he would take away all the pleasure he gave me if I gave myself any relief. Not like it was hard to get him to give it to me. He seemed to only ever be a phone call or text message away.

Sighing, I rolled over and picked up my phone from where I'd tossed it on the nightstand when I'd entered my room. No messages. Damn.

I lay in bed for long minutes debating on sending one to Master or waiting for him to contact me. I wanted him to make sure he knew exactly how much I enjoyed our time together, but I didn't want him to realize how much I was coming to need him. If he knew how much I thought about him and everything he did to me, I'm sure he would run screaming for the hills. No sane man wants a woman like that.

Then again, I'd told him about my addiction and he'd handled it in stride, just like everything else. I wish I had a fraction of that control, that confidence in everything I did. Not once had I noticed a hesitation in anything he did to me.

I still didn't know anything personal about him except that he had brown hair and a delicious body hiding under those extremely well-fitted clothes I caught glimpses of. I guessed it was time to start pushing for my questions that he'd promised me early on, but had stopped asking as I grew more comfortable with our situation.

Chapter 18

John

She'd run out after I came... right after. I'd barely rolled over when she'd opened the door to the dressing room. I tried my best not to let her know I was fully awake. Not a chance in hell would I fall asleep after something so amazing. Relaxed? Yes. Asleep? Please. I wasn't that kind of man. I had had plans to give her more to remember the night by — until she'd slipped from the bed and run out. As soon as the door clicked shut behind her, I snatched up her panties before retreating through the door on the opposite side to watch her in the cameras. Watching her, I pressed the button to let the cleaning crew know to clean the room. They moved quickly entering the room almost immediately after I pressed the button. Intrigued, I watched as Alix battled with herself before reentering the room. The cleaning crew had already slipped back out after removing all the bedding.

I wasn't sure what she was looking for, but she'd seemed determined to find whatever it had been. Seeing that the room had been cleaned, she turned to leave. Quickly throwing on my jeans sans underwear, I stalked after her, pulling on my shirt as I went. I was only feet behind her in the hallway; she could've easily turned around and seen me, but she didn't. Once we were outside, she tensed up and I knew she must've heard my footfalls. Dodging behind a car and following at a more discreet distance, I made sure she made it to her car safely. With her looking for something, I didn't want her to go off searching around the club and ending up somewhere she shouldn't.

Peeking around a car, I watched and waited until she left the parking lot and turned down a side street, disappearing from my view. When I returned to the club, the woman at the front informed me that the cleaning crew found something in the sheets as they were putting them in the wash. As she held up a small, clear bag with Alix's pearl necklace in it, I immediately knew what Alix had been looking for. Pride flared inside me that she cared enough to look for them while at the same time thoughts of how I could return them to her started to fly through my head. Taking the bag from the greeter, I quickly returned to my room and gathered my things before leaving. I was half-tempted to drive by Alix's house, but I talked myself out of it. Or I thought I had, until I found myself turning down her street. Slowing down so I could get a good look at the house, I assured myself that she had indeed made it home safely. Her bedroom light was on and through the sheer curtains over the window I could see her walking around in the room.

Driving away, I fought with myself; I wanted to stay and watch her, but I didn't. I went back to my apartment and threw my bag next to the door to be dealt with later. Pulling the bag with the necklace from my pocket, I went to my computer and turned it on. As it booted up, my mind drifted.

I knew that if Alix ever found out about my habit of following her, it would freak her out. I knew I should stop, yet I didn't. I couldn't. I'd never followed a woman before. I'd never felt the compulsion, desire, *need* to make sure a woman was safe. Even though I knew it was wrong and creepy, I couldn't fight it. In a way, it was why Alix and I were so perfect. We each had a huge character flaw, one that most people would probably have a hard time seeing past, but together we were perfect. I could help her with her addiction and she was my addiction. Having her in my arms every night, in my bed every morning, would calm the beast inside me.

It was simply a matter of making her see the same logic. It was crazy. *I* was crazy. While I was in complete control of every other aspect of my life, this one woman was my weakness. The more I learned about her, the deeper in her mind I dug, the more I wanted to know, the deeper I wanted to get. It was never enough.

Some of the things I did for her were illegal. I could lose my license. I could get arrested. It didn't matter — I'd give it all up for her. What exactly it was about her that made me lose my hard-won control, I couldn't put my finger on. Maybe that was why I was so obsessed. I wanted to know why she was the one woman who had found the way behind my walls. Maybe the obsession would fade once I figured it out.

It was the same conversation I always had in my head after meeting with Alix. I wanted her. I hated myself for the level of want I had for her. I hated the obsessive need I had for her. I wanted to figure it out and get rid of it. Could I figure out my faulty mind and still want Alix? Or would I grow tired of her once everything came to light? Would *she* want *me* if she knew about me?

The only way to find out would be to keep digging into my own subconscious while also finding out more about Alix. Every time I thought I knew who she was, she surprised me with a new, undiscovered layer she'd kept hidden. Just like I'd never suspected she was into the same kink I was. What a pleasant surprise that had been.

What I really needed to do was get her to start asking her questions after our sessions instead of running out on me. The questions she asked revealed more that she realized. It wasn't about her getting to know me. They let me see what interested her, what parts of me she wanted to know — or was it simply the BDSM aspects she wanted to know about? A question was never just a question.

My computer beeped, alerting me to incoming emails. I had quite a few to read through. I had a secretary to help handle patients, but the current system wasn't working well. I had more work than I could handle alone. I needed someone to handle incoming new patient calls and emails. Unbeknownst to my current secretary I'd put out word that I was unofficially looking for a replacement. I had a few applicant emails that I needed to sort through as well.

It wasn't a task I looked forward to. I needed someone who could handle odd requests without getting freaked out or sharing their personal opinion with clients. The last thing I needed was an upset client because my secretary told them what interested them was weird, gross, or who knows what else. Privacy was extremely important to all of my clients as well as my business.

Leaning back in my chair, I started browsing through some of the applicants. I really needed someone to handle the phone calls. A lot of my appointments were being scheduled for out-of-the-office meetings, but I needed someone that had all my in-office and out-of-

office appointments in one place so they didn't overlap or have me running all over town.

Two hours passed as I filtered through résumé. I'd narrowed it down to my top ten. Normally I skipped the name portion of the application as sex and race didn't matter at all to me. What mattered is what experience the person had and if I thought they would be a good fit based on previous work experience. However, once I narrowed it down, I glanced at the names just to see whom I might be dealing with. When my ex's name came up, I froze. I hadn't heard from Mariah in a very long time. Our relationship had ended amicably, from how I remembered it; however, I didn't expect to find her applying for employment with my practice. She knew exactly what type of practice I had. I was just starting my business when we'd been together, the same specialty I still practiced. It had bothered her that I was in the middle of other people's sex lives... literally. Initially she thought I exaggerated or made up stories about exactly what I did when I was with clients.

Until one day I was running really late for lunch with her. She was in the waiting room along with two of my clients who were waiting for one-on-one sessions with me. The two women had been sharing what the sessions with their significant others were like. Needless to say Mariah wasn't so happy about it. I'd never lied to her, never kept the truth from her, but she felt like I had because she hadn't believed what I had been telling her. Not that I physically got involved with my clients, but it didn't matter to her. She couldn't handle the fact that on a daily basis I saw other women (and men) nude and doing sexual things to one another.

It didn't take long from the time that she found

out until we broke up for good. She'd begged and pleaded multiple times for me to give her another chance. A few times I actually had. She was a good sub, and at the time that was all I needed from a woman in my life. Sadly, every time ended the same way — with a huge fight full of accusations that were all based on bullshit. Like that I had to be cheating because I smelled like other women or I always took phone calls in private. Yet another reason why I rarely dated and let women get to know any part of me. They just couldn't handle what I did for a living.

Trying to set aside the personal connection, I carefully analyzed her résumé and surprisingly found that she had the experience that would make her quite a good fit. I knew her personality, so that would be a benefit and make it an easier transition. She definitely would know what type of job she was getting into since she'd seen and heard a lot about it when we'd been together. Then again, throw in the fact that we'd had sex quite a few times and the fact that she knew all about my BDSM side — and it wasn't such a great idea. Still, I starred the email figuring that at least if no one else worked out I would have her to fall back on or get to fill in until I found someone better and less personal. Plus, I would have to deal with the possibility that she was looking to rekindle our relationship after all this time. That was a bridge that I would only cross if I needed to.

As much as I hated wasting time with secretary applicants, I had to. I needed more free time. I wanted more time to spend with Alix, not just at the club, but outside of our room — without the blindfold. I needed to find a way to gently get away from this looming secret. She would find out one way or another. Secrets never lasted forever and my identity wasn't one to just have her stumble upon. It could wreck everything, make her run, if it didn't happen just right.

Just as I was about to close my laptop, my email dinged with a different tone than normal. It was Alix. She was looking to talk to her counselor. I figured after the busy day she'd had, plus the time we'd spent together, she would be fast asleep, but she was looking to talk to someone. That wasn't a good sign. I would much rather have left her too exhausted to stay awake once she got home.

Opening the chat window, I settled in and hoped the chat would go better than the last time.

Counselor21: Good evening. How are you?

BadKitty2: How do you think I'm doing? It's the middle of the night on a Saturday and I'm here talking to you.

Counselor21: Anywhere else you'd rather be?

BadKitty2: Of course.

Counselor21: And where would that be?

BadKitty2: Naked in bed with my master.

Counselor21: So things have been going well then?

BadKitty2: Somewhat.

Counselor21: What is keeping you from being with him tonight?

I had to know what made her run out of the room like it was on fire. She didn't know it was me behind the computer, but it gave me the chance to find out what she wasn't willing to talk to me about in person.

When she didn't respond for a few moments, I tried again.

Counselor21: What makes you say that things are only

somewhat going well? Have you ventured farther into the BDSM world since the last time we talked? Did things not go as you'd expected?

BadKitty2: I have explored more. Surprisingly, I discovered that it is much more than I first thought.

Counselor21: How so?

BadKitty2: Well… I haven't masturbated in quite a while. I don't even think about it.

Counselor21: Do you think about your next meeting with your master? Or the next time he will give you release? Does he do that? Is there a sexual aspect to your relationship?

BadKitty2: I think about him. Sometimes I try to anticipate what will occur the next time we are together, but not specifically the release he may or may not give me. He has brought me to the edge of release, but not allowed me to have it when I have done something that doesn't please him.

BadKitty2: That's not how it might sound. It's always little things. He makes me want to be better. The way I feel when I'm with him is so freeing. I don't have to think, don't have to worry about the little things in life. I know that he is going to take care of me, he is going to make sure I get everything I need right then.

Counselor21: That sounds like things are much better than you initially made them seem. What am I missing?

BadKitty2: I don't know his name. I'm not allowed to see his face. I'm beginning to wonder what he is hiding.

Counselor21: Are you afraid he has some horrible deformity or something like that?

BadKitty2: I don't care what he looks like. I just want to know. It was fun and different and added to the whole scene at first, but I want to be able to have a face and name to put to him in my dreams.

Counselor21: Have you told him this?

BadKitty2: No.

Counselor21: Why not? If it is something that bothers you so much. Would you be willing to stop seeing him if he said no?

BadKitty2: It is what I have been going round and round about. I can't say. I can only say that I have given it serious thought.

Counselor21: Beyond the name and face issue, what else is causing you to say that things are only okay?

BadKitty2: He refuses to have sex.

Counselor21: And that is a bad thing?

BadKitty2: Yes. No. I don't know. It's weird. I've never had a man tell me he didn't want to have sex. I even went as far as accusing him of being gay to see if I could propel him past whatever hiccup there seems to be or find out what the truth was.

Counselor21: How did he react to that?

BadKitty2: Not well. Well, he proved that he certainly loves pussy. I don't think I can ever forget the way he proved that he does indeed love pussy or the orgasm that I got from it.

BadKitty2: I feel a little like I'm over-sharing here.

Counselor21: Not at all.

BadKitty2: Things got more physical between us than they ever had before, but I still had to push him to let me touch him. Do things to him.

Counselor21: Do you think that maybe he wants to keep the first time the two of you go all the way for when you know who he is?

BadKitty2: I doubt it. He has made no indication that he plans to ever reveal his name or face to me.

That statement made me realize how little she knew about me.

Chapter 19

Alix

After a few more exchanges with the counselor, I finally logged off. He spent the last bit reassuring me that I needed to open the lines of communication with Master. Easier said than done, Sir. Easier said than done.

It's not that I didn't want to talk to him. I did. I wanted to know everything there was to know about him. It was finding the time to bring up topics I knew wouldn't go over well. Or at least I expected wouldn't be taken well.

That's why I'd run from the room after he got off. I realized just how much more I was coming to want and that he never made any mention or indication that he wanted more. It had taken pacing my bedroom for hours to finally sort through all my feelings.

I wanted Master in a way that I'd never wanted anyone else, yet knew very little about him. I didn't need to know all the details of his life to know that I wanted more. I needed more. Not just his name. Not just to see his handsome face. I knew he was handsome. I'd been granted the pleasure of feeling his face a single, unforgettable time.

Shutting down my computer, I crawled into bed and lay in the dark staring at my phone. I had Sunday and Monday off so at least I could sleep in.

The night had been so incredible I didn't want it to end. My only regret was not letting Master recover more before I'd left. I couldn't help it at the time. Maybe if I had I would have remembered to retrieve my pearls. Hopefully he would return them to me the next time I saw him.

Talking to the counselor had been my way to try to calm my mind. It was hard for me to open up, especially to a faceless person, about such private things. Although it had originally been what appealed to me, it also made it a bit awkward. It was the first time I really, truly felt better after talking to him. It was also the first time I opened myself up so much.

Finally feeling calm enough, I sent Master a text letting him know that I had gotten home okay and that I was sorry for running out so quickly. Staring at the phone, I waited for a reply for a full twenty minutes before turning off the phone.

Time passed painfully slow until I finally fell into a fitful sleep. When I woke up a few short hours later, I felt no more rested than when I'd fallen asleep, but I had managed to have a dream that I wouldn't be forgetting for quite some time.

I had dreamed that Master J was John from the hotel. John, J... It totally worked. My subconscious had to be playing games on me. The chances of them being one and the same were practically impossible. How many people had names that began with the letter J?

In my dream I hadn't exactly seen the man's face, but he had John's hands with Master's voice. His body had felt the same as Master's while looking like John's. His hair was cut like John's but the same color as my glimpse of Master's.

What a mind-fuck.

It had only been a dream, but it had felt so real. Just thinking about the way his hands had touched me, made me feel, had shivers running down my back. I knew if I checked, my panties would be damp. My fingers tingled with the thought of how easily they could slip between my thighs and ease the ache the naughty dream had created.

Throwing back the covers, I jumped from the bed. It was too much temptation to stay bundled up with the remnants of the dream floating around my head. Laundry is never sexy, so I decided that's what I would do. Quickly gathering the random clothing items scattered around the room, I hefted the overfull basket onto my hip. Once in the laundry room, I dropped it on the floor with a loud clap of plastic meeting tile.

Sadly it only took a few minutes to get the first load into the washer, leaving me with nothing to do for at least thirty minutes. Glancing around the kitchen, right off the laundry room, I thought the dishes needed to be done.

And that's how the entire day went. Desperately hunting for something to do. As soon as that was done, I would again be left searching. While slightly aggravating, it also resulted in a closet and dresser filled with clothes and a clean house.

Falling on my bed, exhausted, I finally let my mind drift to the night before and the time I spent under Master's hand. Surprised, I jumped off the bed and retrieved my phone to find that I had numerous unread messages and even a missed call. Apparently Master didn't like when I didn't answer him right away.

I quickly scrolled through the messages, barely reading them, until I got to the most recent message from Master. He went from nice, to upset, to worried. I'm sure he wasn't going to be happy when I told him why I hadn't responded all night or day. I had no real reason. I had never turned my phone off since we'd started texting me. I was normally afraid of missing a call from work or a message from him, but I hadn't been thinking clearly when I'd gone to bed the night before. Plus, I was a bit upset that I hadn't heard right back from him. He had probably been sleeping, but that hadn't crossed my mind then. Then when I woke up I'd simply been so busy trying to keep myself from giving into the burning fire in my gut begging for me to give in and ease the need for release.

Sighing, I sat down on the edge of the bed and sent Master a message apologizing for being unreachable all day and explaining that I had been cleaning and taking care of the things that were neglected during the work week. My phone started ringing immediately. Putting it up to my ear, I answered with a meek, "Hello."

"Cleaning? I was ignored for a pile of dirty clothes and a toilet that needed scrubbing?" Master's voice rumbled through the line, clearly upset.

"I'm sorry. I didn't mean to. Last night took a lot out of me and by the time I fell into bed I wasn't thinking and turned off my phone. Then today I was running around trying to get everything done and keep my mind off the crazy dreams I had last night. I wasn't purposefully ignoring you. I was actually thinking of you since my dream involved you, just not that you might be looking for me, since I didn't hear my phone going off." A defeated breath escaped me. It was a complete accident, but I knew that I had caused him to worry unnecessarily and that was my fault. I knew that I would have some making up to do.

"I didn't know that. Last thing I knew, you'd run from the room — from me. I woke up this morning to a message, but then was unable to reach you all day. I was afraid something had happened since I don't know why you were still up hours after our time together. Apparently I hadn't given you everything you needed or you would've been too relaxed to stay up for hours after you ran out on me." While his voice wasn't as angry, it was still tight.

"I will make it up to you, sir. I promise." I picked at my cuticles, not knowing how to placate him.

"Damn right you will," he nearly yelled through the phone. "I have something of yours as well. I was going to give them back to you, but now I'm not so sure I should. I'm so easily forgotten."

"My pearls. Sir, I want them back. I'll come to you right now. Anything, sir." I couldn't fight the rejected feeling that overcame me. Logical or not, I needed those pearls more than I needed my next breath. I might have more questions than I could write down for him, but I didn't want to lose the connection we had over something so stupid.

"Meet me at the club. You have one hour." Master hung up the phone before I could respond.

Jumping off the bed, I immediately stripped out of my clothes and pulled on a skimpy pair of panties and a bra before covering up with a trench coat. My favorite five-inch heels were slipped on before I stepped out of the house. There was no reason to get dressed. Master never saw me dressed and I didn't want to waste any time putting on clothes only to take them off when I got to the club.

As I drove to the club, I pulled out my hair tie and fluffed my hair. I still had on the leather collar from the night before. I had tucked the chain into the collar so it stayed out of the way but I hadn't removed it. Hopefully Master would be able to tell that I was still fully invested in our relationship, even though I had slipped up and not answered my phone. There were a lot of things I wasn't sure about, but I realized that even though I had entertained the idea of leaving Master because I didn't know his name or face, I couldn't do it.

I didn't need to know his name or see his face to let him teach me how to be a stronger person — how to fight the constant internal battle that went on. The day hadn't been easy, but it certainly hadn't been as rough as it could've been, and I hadn't given in to the strong desire to masturbate. Hell, it had been days since I'd even had that temptation and that was something I could brush aside. It was too important.

The amount of freedom I could gain from finally conquering my demons would extend to every part of my life. I had once had that freedom, or I thought I had. The life I lived after rehab wasn't life. I lived in constant fear that something would set me back. Even trying to avoid it with every blink of my eye, I still tripped and fell back in to old habits.

The control that I was gaining from being under Master's careful, knowledgeable hand showed me that I never really had defeated it before. I'd simply put it in a box that would spring open again whether I wanted it to or not. Master was showing me that I could leave it there in the open, acknowledge it and continue on without letting it take over my life. I still had a long way to go and I wasn't ready to lose the man who had created the unusual, but successful path in my brain.

After spending hours trying to clear the murky water in my brain about Master's and my situation, I had made very little progress. This one falter cleared the water so quickly it was staggering. I needed Master and I would do anything to make him see that.

When I arrived at the club, I knew I wasn't looking my best. The only make-up I had on was what was left from the night before and a day of cleaning. As I walked through the parking lot, I realized I should have showered since I probably didn't smell the best. Oh well, too late. I ran my fingers through my hair taking care of a few knots. The man at the door, let me in without a word. I handed over my purse to the woman inside and strode down the hall, determination radiating off me. Each step brought me that much closer to a pivotal moment.

With the final steps to the dressing room, I unbuttoned my jacket. As soon as the door was open, I dropped my jacket onto the chair and was kneeling on the floor before it could click closed behind me.

"Hmm. Didn't waste any time, did you?" Master's voice came from across the room. There was a current of pleasure in his tone.

"No, sir. I got here as fast as I could." I kept my eyes locked on the ground even though I knew I could easily look up and finally get that glimpse of his face I craved. That wasn't now I wanted it though. I wanted him to want me to know more about him. The black silk cloth was draped in front of my eyes as a pair of bare feet stepped into my sight. The view had my back straightening. It wasn't what I was used to. He always had shoes on. I couldn't help but admire the well-groomed manly feet and the jeans that brushed the ground.

Before he could say anything or wrap the silk around my head, I bowed and brought my lips to the top of each foot. It was the first way to show him I was grateful for him giving me the opportunity to make up for my idiocy.

"Stop," Master barked. "You are *never* to kiss my feet. That's a slave thing and I don't want a slave. I want a woman who can stand next to me while submitting to my desires."

"I have made an error and I want to apologize, sir," I murmured. "I just want to make you happy."

"I have shown you how to make me happy. I might not be all that happy at this exact moment, but you are never below me in such a way that you bow to me like that again. You submit to me because you choose to. You give the control of our time together to me. You are worth more than that. Those lips are too perfect to be touching dirty things that touch the ground."

As he spoke, he wrapped the blindfold around my eyes. Once it was tied, he buried his hand in my hair, tugging my head back before his lips came forcefully down on mine. His tongue plunged into my mouth to touch and taste. Yanking his mouth away moments later, his forehead pressed to mine. Our breath mixing as his bare chest brushed against the material of my bra.

"Don't ever ignore your phone again." His grip in my hair tightened and his other arm wrapped around my waist. The tightening of his arm brought me firmly chest to chest with him. He had gotten to his knees in front of me, it was the only way he could possibly be touching me the way he was. Tilting my head to the side, he left open-mouthed, wet kisses along the column of my neck as he continued to hold me close.

"I won't, sir," I said as he sucked and licked at the sensitive skin where my neck met my shoulder.

After a few more kisses, he rested his cheek against mine. The rough stubble across his cheek scraped my face. "I shouldn't tell you this, but I was so God-damn worried you had decided you were done with me."

"Master? Why would you think that?" I didn't know what would make him jump to that conclusion since I'd sent him a message to apologize for running out on him before heading to bed.

"I...just did. After the way you left last night, and then not hearing from you all day. My mind went wild trying to figure out what had happened," he released a shaky breath, holding me closer.

I didn't fully understand why he was reacting the way he was. I understood that I had been wrong for not answering all day, but his reaction seemed a bit extreme. Then again, nothing was even remotely normal in our relationship, if it could even be called that.

"Let me make it up to you, Master." It was all I could do. This side of Master, while touching, was freaking me out. I was used to the untouchable, all-knowing version and I wanted it back. That was the man I needed and I would do whatever I had to in order to get him back.

Chapter 20

John

To say that I freaked out when I didn't hear from Alix for almost twenty-four hours would be an understatement. I drove past her house multiple times, was even late to meet clients because I needed to see if I could get a glimpse of her. I hadn't even seen curtains moving as she walked past. It was much easier to see where she was at night, and as soon as I was done with clients for the day I was back to her house.

My brain was throwing together every possible scenario, and the one that stuck together the best was that she had decided that she was done with me because she didn't know enough about me. It took me a long time to convince myself that ringing her doorbell and announcing who I was wasn't the right way to reveal my identity. It would only make the situation worse.

When she finally texted, I was in such a whirlwind of emotions, anger was the first to come out. Then when I saw her strip so quickly and kneel in our room at the club, relief had flooded me and I nearly broke down. Kneeling in front of her with my arms wrapped around her, I tried to rebuild some of my composure before I revealed too much of myself to her. I knew it looked like I was overreacting. All day I had been dealing with the idea that the woman I cared for more than anything in my life possibly no longer wanted anything to do with me. Alix had come to mean more to me than simply the woman I needed to know everything about and protect, she had become the woman who could break me.

Having her kiss my feet had been the final straw. No woman should feel like she needed to kiss the feet of her master, like she worshiped the ground he walked on. While I thought of Alix as my submissive, she had more control over me than I did her. She was beauty personified and I was no where near worthy of her worship.

I had to tell her who I was. I had to try to find a logical way to get through the crazy web of deceit I'd created around us.

First though, I had to ensure she and I were all right. Everything had to be perfect before I dared to reveal a secret that was going to be hard enough to get through as it was. Pulling back from her, I released her hair and body from my grip. The loss of warmth was disappointing, but I had to get my head where it needed to be so I could give her what she needed while centering myself at the same time.

"Stand." I lifted her chin with a finger. She obeyed showing me the delicious scraps of material covering my favorite parts of her body. "Strip." I dropped my hand and stepped back so I could fully appreciate her skin as it was revealed. "I hope you are ready."

"Yes, sir," her steady voice responded immediately.

"Good." I brushed her hair over her shoulders letting my fingers drag over her skin as I did it. That's when my eyes landed on the leather collar around her neck and the silver chain still attached. "Still wearing my collar, are you?"

"I couldn't bring myself to take it off, sir." She

lifted her chin proudly so I could see the collar better.

The smile that jumped to my lips wouldn't be denied. There was nothing sexier than seeing her spirit despite having a blindfold on and being completely nude. "I understand, Precious, that it was a mistake. An error, if you will. However, I am still going to punish you so that you don't forget anytime soon." I licked my lips as my eyes ate up every inch of silky skin on display. Reaching up, I tugged on the chain to release it from the way she'd kept it tucked up and out of her way. With the chain wrapped around my hand, I led her across the room to the St. Andrew's cross in the corner. I hadn't yet tied her up to it, but it seemed the perfect time to use it. Skimming my hands over her shoulders and down her arms until I reached her wrists, I circled them with my fingers before lifting them above her head. "Stay," I breathed into her hair.

Stepping to the stand near the wall, I removed four long strands of pearls I had bought for just such an occasion. Returning to Alix, I wrapped a strand around each wrist, securing her to the cross before doing the same to her ankles.

"You are tied with pearls. Pull, struggle, fight at all and you'll break them. Break them and it all stops. Understood?" Unable to help myself, I fisted her hair so I could pull her head to the side and sink my teeth into that ultra-sensitive skin at the base of her neck. Feeling her body tense and the grunt of pain she fought to hold back as I bit her had my cock swelling in my jeans. I'd been in the process of changing into my suit when she'd showed up. Not willing to make her wait, I'd come to her in just my jeans and feeling her skin repeatedly against my own made me wish I had done so before.

"I understand, sir," Alix grunted as I released her hair.

Placing a soft kiss against the angry red marks from my teeth, I stepped away from her again. All of her was on display and I planned to take advantage of it. There would be no rushing. I was going to make sure she knew down to the smallest grain of her being that she was mine and only mine. Looking at the wall of treasures, I debated on which one would be the best to use. A glint of something silver caught the corner of my eye. Turning my head, a dark smile took over as I knew I had found exactly what the night's pleasure was going to be. The small metallic object was perfect.

Without getting too close, I reached out and let the sharp points of the Wartenburg's wheel roll across Alix's shoulders. The sharp inhale let me know she felt the tiny points exactly how I wanted her to. They left a beautiful pattern behind on her skin. Lowering my hand, I started at the base of her spine. As the spikes worked their way along her back, she groaned and arched her back, but didn't tug on her delicate restraints. After giving her a moment to wonder where I was going to go next, I started at her hip and followed the curves of her body. The sides of her breast were going to be sensitive anyway, but I pressed harder, letting the points dig in a bit more. "Oh!" Alix yelped, but still didn't struggle.

After repeating the treatment to the other side of her body, I put the wheel back on the stand. As pleasing as it was to see the dots left behind on her skin, I wanted to see more. Opening the bottom drawer of the stand, I pulled out the carefully-wound rope. As I undid the ties, the free end of the rope slapped against the ground — teasing Alix with what was to come next.

Once I had the entire length of the rope free, I

closed the distance between Alix and me. The warmth of her back against my chest, the swell of her ass pressed against my throbbing cock had me dropping my lips to her neck. Not lifting my head, I spoke against her skin. "This is something new. I will be right here. Speak to me as I work so I know you are doing all right."

"Yes, sir. What would you like me to talk about?" She tilted her head away to give me better access to her throat.

"Ask questions and I'll ask you questions." I knew it'd be the perfect time for us to get to know each other better as I showed her one of my favorite things.

"I can do that." She smiled. "Will I still be in the pearls?"

"No. I will take them off in just a moment. Don't move unless I tell you to, though." Running my palms up her raised arms, I slowly undid the pearl restraints. As each came undone, I placed them around her neck, replacing the strand she'd left behind. Once she was released, I started with the rope. It wasn't a fast process to get her tied up the way I wanted, but if I kept her distracted and talking there was no reason she couldn't do it.

"Is this going to hurt?" she asked after I'd wrapped the rope around her stomach a few times, knotting it as I went.

"No. If it does, tell me right away," I reassured her as I kept working on the intricate knots.

"Will you ever tell me your name?" She wasted no time getting to the questions I knew were coming.

"One day."

"Can I see your face?" She didn't hesitate at all.

"Soon." I still hadn't figured out how, so I

couldn't say more than that.

"Have I seen you before? You know, outside of here?"

"You have." I smiled. She was trying to piece everything together.

"Have we spoken?"

"No." I knew that'd give me away almost instantly. Not all that many men had the British accent I was unable to get rid of. Plus, she'd heard my voice so much I was sure she'd be able to identify me just from that.

"What is so special about your job that you won't tell me what it is?" she asked after a moment of thought.

"Let's just say that not everyone likes what I do and I didn't want that to get in the way of us getting to know each other."

"Are you a lawyer? No one likes lawyers." She smirked even as she asked, which made me laugh.

"No. Not a lawyer. I can't stand them either. Unless they are saving me from angry clients." As soon as the words left my mouth, I knew I'd let slip something I hadn't meant to. Instead of letting it show, I kept working with the rope as if I'd meant to share that I had clients.

"I can only imagine. I know I've dealt with some horrible clients. Thankfully they can't really come after me for anything, but in other situations I could see how they would be absolutely the last person I wanted to deal with." She sighed as I tightened a knot, securing one of her wrists to her body. Her eyes fluttered closed for a brief moment before slowly opening again. Her voice was noticeably relaxed when she asked, "I thought I was getting a punishment — this doesn't feel like punishment."

"No, not a punishment, Precious. I would never lay a hand on you in anger. This is not a time for discipline, but a reminder of all that we have together." As I secured her other wrist, effectively restraining her, I felt a sense of calm wash over me. Knowing that I was in control of her body in every aspect gave me the same rush that a sub got from handing over their control. The adrenaline rush knowing I was in charge — I am the master.

I could see Alix was in subspace from the slowed blink of her eyes and relaxed body. Scooping her into my arms, I carried her to the bed. Brushing my hand over her cheek, I smiled back when a lazy smile tilted her beautiful lips. Slowly, I began to remove the bondage from her — it had served it's purpose. Simply having rope restrict a submissive's movements was all it took to most to subspace. Seeing the rope release her, but leave behind the rugged marks was quite possibly the sexiest thing I'd ever seen on Alix. A sign of her submission etched on her skin for everyone to see.

Once all of the rope was removed, I made sure all four pearl necklaces were still around her neck before sitting next to her on the bed. Placing one of her hands on the necklaces, I made sure she knew they were there.

"These are to replace the one you left behind. I am now going to remove the leather version, as I'd much rather see my woman draped in pearls than strapped down in leather." I carefully took the leather collar from her neck. Even though she had marks all along her torso from the rope, I was still slightly disappointed that the leather collar didn't leave additional marks on her. She could never have too many marks on her to show everyone that she was mine. Sadly the rope marks would only last for a few hours at most. The marks left on her mind would last much longer. There is nothing as special as the first time you let someone restrict your movement. The fact that you trust someone enough to tie you up and that the person doing the tying up has earned that level of trust, creates a unique bond.

I didn't know if Alix understood everything I was trying to show her, but I was willing to illustrate again if she missed anything. I wanted her to ask questions that came to her mind, not me telling her things that didn't matter to her.

Alix simply nodded when I told her about the pearls — still flying in subspace. After admiring her beauty and the red marks on her creamy skin for a few minutes longer, I flicked off the lights and joined her in the bed. Tucking her close to my chest, her small palm lifted to rest above my pounding heart as a relaxed sigh brushed against my skin. My cock was throbbing for attention, but that wasn't part of the plan. The lesson of the night was about control and I wasn't going to let mine slip because my dick wanted in her tight pussy.

Releasing the knot on the blindfold, I removed it from her eyes. Wetness met my chest when the silk moved. Tears? Immediately, I sat up so I could rub my thumbs under her eyes. Sure enough, there were more tears there.

"Precious, why are you crying?" I asked stroking her hair.

"It was just so beautiful." She gave a short laugh and reached up to swipe at her face, but I beat her.

Using my lips, I removed every tear I could find. It was my pleasure to kiss tears off her.

"Can I ask one favor?" Alix asked, reaching up to hold my wrist as I cupped her cheek.

"Anything." The single word was out before I even thought it through.

"Will you hold me until I fall asleep?" she whispered.

"Absolutely." I lay down and pulled her close again. Her breath on my chest, her weight resting against me, relaxed me. As I ran my hand over and through her hair, I found myself fighting to keep my eyes open. When her breathing slowed and deepened, I told myself it was time to get up. The scent of her was wrapped around me, the heat of her body seeped into mine and I was captive to her unintentional spell. Before I could put up a good fight, I was fast asleep with my woman wrapped in my arms.

Chapter 21

Alix

Rolling over, I realized that I was not in my own bed. There was too much space. The sheets were softer than the ones I owned. Sitting up, I looked around the barely-lit room only to realize that I was still in the room where Master and I had played. I couldn't believe that I had slept — normally I dozed off, but never for more than a few minutes. From the way fogginess in my head, a few hours had to have passed. Feeling around the massive bed, I found I was alone in it. Not what I was hoping for.

I quickly ran my fingers through my tangled hair before climbing from the bed. Since I was nude, I wrapped the sheet around my body and took the few steps needed to bring me to the dressing room, the tail end of the sheet dragging along the floor behind me. I entered the small room hoping that at least my coat was still there, which it was. Although I had left it on the floor, it was hanging on a hook on the wall. Dropping the sheet, I reached for the coat. My own reflection caught my eye in the mirror. The multiple strands of pearls draped around my neck looked incredibly elegant even though they were the only things on my body. In fact, they were so beautiful, I dropped my arm and stared at myself for a few moments. There was more color in my cheeks than normal, my hair sleep-tousled; the faint lines from where Master had wrapped his ropes around me were still visible. I was almost beautiful. Delicately, I ran my fingers up one arm to touch the rope marks. Just seeing them reminded me of Master and the feeling of his hands on me.

A sound from outside the room had me dropping my arm while reaching for my coat with the opposite one. Holding the cold fabric to my chest, I was barely covered when the door to the hallway opened. I dropped my eyes, afraid I was going to be in trouble for taking too long to dress or being out of bed when Master didn't want me to be. Instead, I heard a choking sound which had my eyes shooting up to make sure the person who'd opened the door was okay.

To my horror, it was John. The man I'd dreamed about. The man I'd masturbated thinking about. It was my turn to choke. Instinctively I took a step back toward the other room even as I tried to think of a way to get my jacket on without flashing him. How would I explain what I was doing nude in such a place? Would he tell the people I worked with? He knew who I was! My cheeks burned as embarrassment flared within my soul.

Before I could even fully process the situation or what I was going to do, he took a step forward and reached for me, and I retreated.

"Wait." It was Master's voice. I spun around to find where he was. He had to have entered the room from the other door, but looking around the room, he was no where in sight. Slowly, I turned back to see if John was still there or if maybe I had imagined him. Nope. Still there, hand still extended toward me. As if in slow motion, his mouth opened and Master's voice left John's mouth. "Precious, let me explain."

I stared in horror and stepped back again from the man I'd fantasized about with the Master's voice. It couldn't be. The world was too big for the two to be the same. The chances were slim to none. No. It just wasn't possible. When John took another step toward me, my entire body flamed red. How embarrassing. He'd known who I was the entire time. I had told him about my addiction. He'd caught me masturbating at work. He had more than enough ammunition to completely ruin my life, not just make me lose my job.

Holding out one hand, I slowly shook my head in denial. It just couldn't be.

John took another step closer to me and I retreated again. Realizing that I was still mostly naked, I flipped the jacket over my shoulders, uncaring that I gave him a good, clear view of my entire body as I quickly buttoned it closed — or as quickly as my shaking, fumbling fingers would allow. When I lifted my eyes from the buttons, he had moved closer.

"Alix. Please let me explain. Let's talk about this before you run off," John said softly His hand gently rubbed up and down my arm.

Jerking back from his touch, I rapidly shook my head. I couldn't talk. I couldn't even fully comprehend. Dodging his hand again, I darted around him and out the door in my bare feet. I didn't know where I'd lost my shoes. It didn't matter. What mattered was getting the hell away from the most confusing place I'd ever been. The only thing that had happened since I had first entered the club was that every time I walked through the doors my life got even more confusing and messed up. Rushing past the woman at the entrance, I slammed into the door to the outside only to have it not open and pain to scream down my shoulder from the impact.

"I'm sorry, miss. We have to open the door for you and you have yet to retrieve your purse." The woman spoke calmly as if a woman running for the door was a normal occurrence. Maybe it was, but that didn't matter. I just needed out.

Grabbing my purse as she held it out, I attempted to walk much more calmly toward the door, which thankfully was unlocked as I pressed my hand against it. Once the cool air from outside rushed in against my face, I threw my purse straps over my shoulder and clamped it close to my body as I ran for my car. I didn't care how crazy or strange I looked, I just needed to get away before John or Master or whoever he was came after me. I couldn't handle another run-in with him. I just couldn't.

Thankfully I was able to make it to my car without anyone stopping me. I heard those damn creepy footsteps again, but ignored them, figuring they had to be an echo of my own in the half-full parking lot. Locking the doors of my car, I wasted no time backing out of my spot before speeding the entire way home. A speeding ticket wasn't anything compared to the mess my mind was trying to make sense of, but thankfully I didn't get stopped.

At home, I locked the door after entering. Pressing my back against the thick wood door, I slid down it. My vision was tunneling; all I could see was John's face standing there in the dressing room where I'd stripped numerous times for encounters with Master. It didn't make sense. Breathing rapidly, I tucked my head between my bent knees, folding my arms over my head as I tried to calm myself. A panic attack wouldn't help anything. Finally I was able to get my breathing under control, my vision stopped closing in on me and I leaned back against the door with my eyes closed.

Swallowing hard, it all started to click together.

Master didn't want me to know his name or face. Why? Because I knew who he was. He knew who I was. It made sense why I would want to hide who I was from him, but I couldn't figure out why he would want to hide who he was from me. I didn't know anything about him. Nothing that he hadn't shared with me in our play room, anyway.

He had been in charge of what I knew about him. It didn't make sense.

After several long minutes I was able to convince myself to get up from the floor. I needed to shower. The smell of Master... I mean, John, was all over me. Normally a scent I loathed removing from my body, it just reminded me of the confusing place I was. Everything was a mess. I had to return to work on Tuesday, which left me an entire day to figure out what I was going to do if I saw him while at work. I would see him, I knew that. He seemed to always be around when I was at work. Maybe not always, but it had seemed like I was seeing him more than I normally did. I had thought it was all me making things up, but after the recent turn of events maybe it wasn't so random or made up. He'd known.

That was the part that kept swirling around in my head and I couldn't get over. He.Had.Known.

All the run-ins. All the looks. It all made sense.

What *didn't* make sense was why he was so afraid for me to know.

I went through everything that I could remember over and over as I showered and got my clothes ready for the next day before finally falling into bed. There was absolutely nothing that I could pinpoint as being something I could use against him. It was frustrating, but rehashing the same thing over and over wasn't going to help. A good night's rest was what would.

Lying back in the bed, I tried to relax and convince my brain to shut off so I could find peace in sleep. It didn't happen. Hour after hour passed slowly — one tick of the clock at a time. Eventually my body gave in because it was too exhausted to continue, but all I did was dream of John and Master. It wasn't a sexy mix, but a creepy, frightening mess that had me waking with a scream in my throat and cold sweat running down my back.

After the dream I had, I gave up on getting any more rest. A quick shower with a coffee chaser was the jolt I needed to start my day early. Better to work on my day off than let my mind keep on the path it was going down. No one would question me being in on a Monday. If they did, it was easy to pass off that I was catching up on emails and phone calls. I was salaried anyway, they couldn't complain about overtime since that was a nonexistent dream in my world.

Dressed in a finely-tailored skirt suit, I drove myself to work, cursing traffic and my own horrible idea the entire drive. Once I finally pulled into the hotel parking lot, I breathed a sigh of relief. Work. The one place that was always constant in my life. The one place where I could shut off the overly-critical side of my brain because the creative, artistic side was in demand. It took less than an hour to be elbow-deep in work as if it wasn't my day off. After four hours, I'd nearly forgotten what had happened the night before. Not. It didn't matter how many calls or emails I made or answered, my mind was still partially focused on the events of the night before. Not the pleasurable parts. The parts I wished I could forget. Wash them from my eyes and brain with bleach so I could go back to the mindless, happy pleasure that Master gave me.

I'd thought I needed a face and a name to make things better. Instead, getting both those things had only made everything worse. Those things dropped a bomb, blowing everything into outer space. Things would never be the same. They couldn't be. I was too embarrassed, too confused, to ever be able to act "normal" around him. I would always be the out-of-control sex addict who needed someone to restrain me and tell me what do to in order for me to feel like I had any sense of worth.

Hours passed before I realized that I was still trying to fit into his guidelines. Just to spite him, I found an extra hair tie in a drawer and pulled my hair into a low, messy bun to keep it out of my way. It had nothing to do with him. Not really. It was my way of proving to myself that I was the same as I had been before him.

From what I knew, John didn't show up at the hotel on Mondays anyway so it wasn't like I was doing it for him to see. Yet it gave me a jolt of happiness, knowing that I was defying his command to keep my hair down.

After finally getting through my pile of emails, I had a list of people to call back and things I needed to update in my files for upcoming events. Staring at the list, I had no desire to do any of it. I couldn't get John off my mind. It was just too much for me to push aside. It was like a dream and a nightmare combined and I couldn't find my way out of the confusing, painful mess that everything had become.

Rapidly tapping my fingers on the desk, I tried to think of a way to prove that I didn't need a man who played games with me in my life. I didn't want a man in my life, but somehow or another John *and* Master had found loopholes in my security. They might be one and the same, but in my mind they were two totally different people. John was the physical version of my erotic dreams while Master was the emotional support and path maker. Master wouldn't let me fuck him with my eyes for months on end. Master wouldn't have smiled with a hard-on catching me masturbating. In my mind, John wouldn't have been able to handle a crop or spank me the way that Master had. John wouldn't have kissed me with such a soul-searing kiss or held me so close as I whispered my deepest secrets.

John was the man who was always too good to be with someone like me. Master was the man who knew how to dig through the shy, shamed exterior I'd built around myself to find the sexual, needy woman beneath. I'd never felt as complete, as at ease, as I did when I was in Master's care. John was a man I'd made up numerous theories and ideas about, but in reality I knew little to nothing about the man. Hell, I'd barely learned his name.

No matter how many times or ways I looked at all that I knew, I couldn't combine the two men. They were too different to be the same person until I knew more. I had to find out more somehow.

As if beckoned by my thoughts, John walked up to the receptionist's desk as I lifted my eyes. He wasn't supposed to be at the hotel. He wasn't supposed to be anywhere near me. Even if I thought I was finally starting to find some semblance of understanding of the whole situation, I wasn't ready to have a face-to-face meeting with the man who had thrown my world into a whirlwind in more ways than one.

Chapter 22

John

Alix finding out who I was hadn't happened anywhere close to the way I wished it had. I had slipped away for a few minutes to answer a phone call from a client. In that time, she must have awakened. When I'd returned to the room, I'd been so completely thrown off and surprised to find her standing directly in front of me, barely coving her delicious, nude body with a jacket, that I hadn't been able to think quickly enough. Even though I had run through how I would explain things and make her understand, the pain in her eyes had made me pause too long. By the time I was able to stumble through any sort of explanation she was done waiting. The shove to my chest as she left had felt more like a bullet than her delicate hand. Pain exploded within my mind and chest as she disappeared from my life. I wasn't ready, I'd *never* be ready to lose her.

Somehow I'd managed to gather enough of myself together to rush after her. Even though I may as well have been bleeding out from losing the only thing that mattered in my life, I clumsily tracked her to her car to make sure she was safely away from the club — away from me. As her car escaped my line of sight, I collapsed to the ground, clutching my chest. All the time I'd spent with Alix, everything I'd learned about her, the small details of my life I'd never shared with anyone, but some how managed to let Alix know — everything the two of us shared — flashed through my head making the loss of her shatter every wall I'd ever erected to protect myself. None of it mattered. Not without Alix. Not without the one woman who was able to put up with my dark side. The woman who snuggled deeper into my arms even after I enjoyed bringing her pain. The woman who wanted to experience me as a person more than knowing who I was.

What we had was more than words could express. It was everything you hoped to find in someone, everything someone like me thought they'd ever find.

And I had ruined it.

I was the failure. I let her down. I hurt her and that killed me.

When my legs and back ached from sitting on the asphalt in the parking lot, I pulled myself together enough to retrieve my keys from the club. Feeling as if I were in a cloud, I drove around the city for hours. No destination. No where to be. No one to console me. Worthless, useless…broken.

There was no other way to describe how I felt.

Long after the sun had risen over the city, I made a few circles around Alix's block. Failing to catch a glimpse of her or any sign that she was even home, I went to the hotel. Dragging my feet, I pulled my sorry ass through the lobby. A sudden spark raced up my spine and I straightened as I glanced around.

There was the source. Alix.

Sitting behind her desk, looking like a beaming ray of sunlight, Alix stared at me with a look of shock mixed with anger. Her cheeks blossomed pink briefly before turning red as all signs of shock disappeared. Anger was the only emotion on her face as I walked closer to the window of her office.

I missed the needy look she normally cast in my direction when I returned home after a long day of work. Hell I already missed everything that was soft and inviting about her — that had been yanked away, only to be replaced with a hard, unyielding glare.

As I watched, she leaned back in her chair and a look that I knew intimately slipped over her features. Her plump lower lip disappeared into her mouth as her eyelids drooped to half-mast.

Clenching my hands tightly, I fought the urge to march into her office. My leg muscles tensed with the need to show her what happened when she blatantly broke my rules. Inside my head, I reminded myself repeatedly that it was no longer my right. She wasn't mine anymore. The reminder sparked the pain that had been momentarily forgotten.

Her head collapsed back onto the chair as her rapid breathing made her breasts strain against her suit jacket. Before I even realized it, my feet were moving on their own.   Slipping into her office before kicking the door closed, I watched as her release rolled over her features. It didn't matter that she hid it well, that it would appear like she was simply closing her eyes for a few moments. I knew what she had been doing. What she'd done.

Spinning her chair around, I grabbed her wrist before she could pull it from under her skirt — keeping it in place. Slowly, I dropped to my knees in front of her, bringing me to her level.

"I understand that you are upset. I do. However, I will not stand by while you break my most important rule," I snarled, leaning in so my face was inches from hers.

She swallowed thickly before breaking eye contact and murmuring, "I couldn't help myself."

Lie. It was written all over her face. Yanking her hand from her skirt, I forced three of her fingers into my mouth. The sweet essence left behind on her fingers had my cock jumping to life even as I removed her digits from my lips. "Bullshit. You wanted to push me. You wanted me to see you break my rules."

"Fuck you…John" She tugged her hand from my grip. A light flashed in her eyes letting me know she wanted to call me Master. She'd called me that more than she'd used my actual name.

"Oh, no, Precious. That is where you are wrong. I will be fucking you…and soon. Just be thankful that I have more control and discipline than you do. If I had my way, you'd be bent over this desk with my dick so deep you'd never forget who I am and just how much you mean to me." As the words left my lips, I slid my hands up her arms, slowly trailing over her shoulders until I could cup her bare neck. "We need to talk."

"No," she instantly replied, but made no move to make me release her or break the eye contact.

"We will. I refuse to let you go without fighting for you. Fighting for everything we can have. Everything we both need." I released her neck to rub a thumb over her cheek. "Meet me tonight. You know where and when. I'll be waiting." Not wanting her to forget who she was dealing with, I lowered my mouth to her ear. "I won't fuck you tonight. I'm going to make you beg for it. You know, I can make you beg like you've never begged before. When I finally get my dick in you there will be no doubt who is fucking you, who is your master, who you belong to. Absolutely nothing about my face or name changes who you are to me and just how much I need you."

Pressing a hard kiss to her lipstick-coated lips, I stood and retreated to the door. Just as I stepped through it, I turned and gave her one last look. "Don't disappoint me, Precious."

Like it or not, I was her dominant and I couldn't stand by while she not only purposefully pushed me, but also gave in to her addiction. She was stronger than that. I would make sure she got that in her head when I got her in private. With or without me, she would not be giving into her addiction if I had anything to say about it.

Being that close to her, smelling her, touching her, had been intoxicating. The only thing that kept me from taking things any further was knowing she was still reeling from finding out my identity.

Passing time while waiting until Alix got off work was almost painful. Once it was time, I slipped down the back elevator before speeding to the club. My palms were sweating and my knee bounced the entire drive. She would show. She had to. I refused to entertain the idea that she might not.

In my room where I could see all the screens, I waited for Alix. I had worn my favorite suit just for her. This would be the first time she was with-out her blindfold and I wanted to look my best. As I paced back and forth in the small room, I double-checked my tie and smoothed my shirt, then my coat. Finally, the door slowly opened and Alix slipped inside the dressing room. Staring at the screens, I clasped my hands behind my back so I didn't keep adjusting my suit.

Alix paused for a single moment before stepping into the playroom fully dressed.

Taking a deep, calming breath, I entered through my own door to find my beautiful Precious already on her knees. Her head was down, her silky strands keeping her face from me. Stepping closer, I fought to keep my voice calm as I instructed her to stand.

Her loud, rapid breathing could be heard from my spot across the room. Unexpectedly, her eyes lifted to lock with mine as she slowly stood. Wobbling on her heels for a brief moment, it took her a moment to settle — not once letting her eyes stray from mine.

"Strip." The single word was raspy, torn from my throat.

One button at a time, she loosened the hold the suit coat had on her body before finally shrugging it off her shoulders so it could drift to the floor. Her eyes fluttered closed as she took a deep breath, then in one swift move she untucked her silk tank and pulled it over her head. As her eyes opened, the shirt floated to the ground next to her. It took a moment of fumbling before she was able to unzip her skirt. Releasing the material, it fell from her hips to pool around her heels as it revealed her black garter belt and nude stockings.

Stepping from the discarded clothing, she dropped to her knees again, spreading them wide as I had once asked her to do when I'd wanted to show her off. Her breathing was still audible. The creamy mounds of her breasts rose and fell with her rapid breaths.

Flicking open the single button on my suit jacket, I smiled down at her. "Now that is how I expect to find you in this room."

Tilting her head back, her face was revealed as her hair slid back. A quick toss of her head had her hair flipping over her shoulders. With her hair out of the way, the pearls around her neck were revealed. Seeing where my eyes were locked, she said, "For you, Master."

The most perfect woman was kneeling at my feet with my pearls around her neck as she gazed at me with a look of desire. Not need, desire — desire to please me, to have me give her what she needed.

Sinking my hand into her hair, I forced her head back. "Is that how you truly feel? Do you want everything I can give you? Or is it just a passing fancy?" I hadn't meant to ask the question out loud, but it was out before I could stop it.

"I want to give you everything I am. I want everything you can give me. I want it all." Her body was tense, but her voice left no doubt that she meant every word.

Releasing her hair, I stepped back from her. "Stand, Precious."

As she stood on the skinny heels, she wobbled again.

Reaching out for her elbow to steady her, I asked, "Do your feet hurt?"

"No, sir. I wear them all the time. I'm just nervous." Her answer came quickly, calmly. A small smile tilted her lips briefly.

I'd been dreaming about having her free of the blindfold, seeing me, but having her right in front of me, those eyes burning into mine, was different than I expected. She wasn't looking at me with nerves or confusion. Instead it was confidence that shone brightly in them. If she was really nervous, her unsteady stance was the only sign of it.

Swallowing away my own nerves, I released her elbow. "Undress me."

A low moan filled the silence before her hands lifted to rest upon my shoulders. Her breathing sped up briefly before she managed a few slow breaths. "Yes, sir." Her voice was barely above a whisper. The tiny buttons of my dress shirt were quickly undone by her nimble fingers. After tugging my shirt from my slacks, her delicate hands slid firmly up the line of skin that had been revealed until they spread out at my shoulders. One hand slid up to caress my lips as her tongue dragged over her own.

Pushing her hands under my coat, she shoved the thick material from my shoulders to let it slide down my arms to the floor. Her fingers fisted in each side of my open shirt before she stepped into my body, pressing her skin against mine. Looking into my eyes, her hands moved to wrap around my wrists.

"These are easier to get off if I'm close."

Somehow she had the cuff links out and tossed to the ground in seconds before her hands skimmed up over my shoulders to slip under the loose material and had it following the same path my coat had only moments before.

"You aren't done," I murmured when she stared at my chest for a few moments too long. I didn't know if she was hesitating or appreciating, but either way, it was taking too long.

"I know, sir. I was simply taking in all that I have been unable to before." Her eyes flicked upward for a brief moment as a smile flickered across her lips. Slowly, too slowly, her tiny hands made a path from my shoulders to my waist hitting every nerve ending along the way and making my body feel like it was on fire.

My cock was fully erect, waiting for her to

notice him and give him the attention he thought he deserved. When her hands barely skimmed over him, I grunted in pain. I had waited so long for us to finally be without the blindfold. For her to know exactly who it was she was touching and who was touching her.

"What are you waiting for?" The impatient growl was out before I could stop it when her hands rested upon my hips.

"Patience, Master. You are the one who has made me wait so long to see you and now I feel like I need to fully appreciate every inch I am free to discover. I've begged more than once for this honor and I don't want to rush it." Again her eyes flicked up to meet mine for a brief moment. Her fingers tickled along the top of my pants, causing me to clench my jaw.

I was fighting the need to take over. I'd more than had my chance to enjoy her body; it was her turn. Not that that made it easy.

Finally her fingers tugged on the button that was barely managing to hold back my straining erection. "Hmm, seems like someone else has been eager to be looked upon."

I could see the curl of her lips and the flash of her tongue as she wet her lips while her eyes burned into my crotch.

Her hand swallowed my erection on top of the constricting material of my pants.

"That's not what tonight is about." Gritting my teeth, I removed her hand from my cock. As good as it felt to have her hands on my body, it wasn't enough. I needed to have her skin on mine.

"What *is* tonight about then, if you aren't going to give me what I need?" Her teeth dug into her bottom lip as she quirked an eyebrow at me.

"You. It's always about you." My fingers were in her hair, pulling her snugly against my body as my lips descended to hers as soon as the words were out.

Knowing she could see me, that she knew who I was, made every touch, every caress, more intimate. Finally I had the woman I wanted for so long. She knew who it was that was touching her, who it was that she belonged to. I was no longer her nameless, faceless Master. If I wasn't careful, I'd reveal just how much of myself she already owned and how much she could destroy me if she left again.

Chapter 23

Alix

I couldn't say what made me show up at the club. What made me let him touch me the way he did. Even when we'd been in my office, I had been unable to find it within myself to tell him no. He had seen right through the front I tried to put on.

I had purposefully touched myself, gotten myself off, while he was looking at me. It wasn't hard. I mean, a man with an incredibly sexy body covered in a finely-tailored suit was masturbation material all by itself. Add in everything I knew he could do with his mouth, hands, fingers, and tongue and I was a goner within seconds. It had only taken him a moment to understand what was going on and come after me. If I hadn't just come from playing with my clit, I could have easily come from the dominance he asserted over me in my office. He barely had to touch me to have me trembling in my heels, my pussy weeping for relief that only he seemed to be able to provide. Sure, I could get myself off, but it was nothing like when he was the one in control of it.

I hadn't been prepared to see him when I was at work. He wasn't supposed to be there. As soon as my eyes had landed on him, I knew it didn't matter. It simply wasn't important that I had dreamt about him, that I had touched myself many times while thinking of him. All of it had been in my head; he didn't know any of that. What did matter was that he had known all along where I worked and never once did anything to embarrass me, didn't use the kinky games we played to get me into trouble or fired. I'd even revealed my addiction to him and again, he'd handled it in stride. The only reason I really had to run from him, to never see him again, was embarrassment.

I could deal with a little embarrassment if it meant that I could have more of him. John. He wanted me. He'd even said he needed me. Well, I needed him more.

When he instructed me to meet him at the club, I wanted to deny him. I wanted to deny his control, his dominance over me, but I couldn't. It was what I needed from him. It was what made us work. He knew what I needed even before I did.

Once at the club, I longed to have him take back the control I had inadvertently taken from him. I didn't want it —never really had. I wanted everything he'd taught me, shown me, let me experience while in his care. Having battled my addiction in the past, it had never been as easy as it had been while following John's rules — Master's rules.

Stepping into the play room while still fully dressed had been a blatantly defiant move. I'd hoped it would make him yank off that carefully constructed cover and show me the man beneath. The man I had seen in my office. Strong, in control, but desperate, needy and unafraid to make it known how much he wanted me.

When he entered the room only moments after I did, I knew he had been waiting for me.

Locking eyes with him as he took slow, leisurely steps toward me had my thighs clenching. I'd never seen a man who could wear a suit the way he did. Even though I may have seen it many times, it was different seeing him walk towards *me* with *that* look on his face. It took everything I had to not jump up and run to him; instead I waited for him to instruct me. Seconds or minutes passed as our eyes burned into each others. The first time we saw each other in such an intimate setting — a place where we were alone.

A few short words were all it took to have me stripping myself and then him. There was nothing I wanted more in the world than to have my hands on his skin, his scent enveloping me. When I was finally able to touch the bulging cock that had been simply begging for my attention, my knees grew weak. It would've been so easy to drop to my knees and beg to take him in my mouth, but he stopped me, saying that tonight wasn't about him.

It was about me.

Yeah, well, we would see about that. Submissive, yes. Stupid, no. I would let him do whatever he wanted as long as I got my hands on that hot, pulsing flesh hiding behind his zipper. Too much anticipation, too much desire burned through me to not get my hands on it.

After everything we'd been through — secrets, blindfold, addiction — and more — we were finally to a place where it was just him and me. I refused to let this chance pass me by.

We might both have our own, unique, pretty fucking crazy quirks, but we were everything no one else would ever be...

To Be Continued...

Also Available by Rachael Orman

Cravings Series
Lost Desires (Cravings 0.5 - John's Patients #1)
Addict (Cravings #1 – John & Alix Part 1)
Fiend (Cravings #2 – John & Alix Part 2) –
Coming Early 2015

The Her Series
Her Ride (Ryan & Elli's Story)
Her Journey (Melia & Patrick's Story)

The Yearning Series
Yearning Devotion (Gwen, McKayla & Cole -
Part 1)
Yearning Absolution (Gwen, McKayla & Cole -
Part 2)

Other Works:
Loneliness Ebbs Deep - Short Story (Co-written
with Adrian J. Smith)

53204008R00121

Made in the USA
San Bernardino, CA
09 September 2017